Troubadour's Storybag

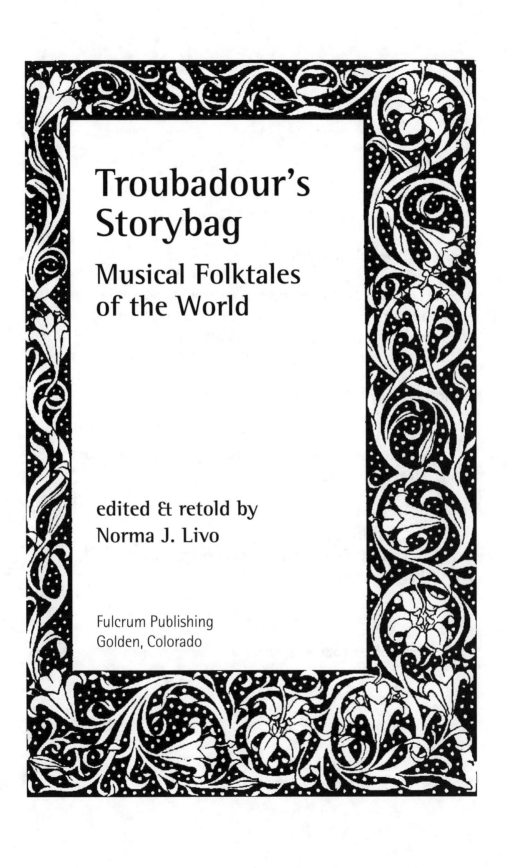

Troubadour's Storybag

Musical Folktales of the World

edited & retold by
Norma J. Livo

Fulcrum Publishing
Golden, Colorado

Library of Congress Cataloging-in-Publication Data

Livo, Norma J., 1929–
    Troubadour's storybag : musical folktales of the world / edited
  and retold by Norma J. Livo.
        p.   cm.
    Includes index.
    ISBN 1-55591-953-7
    1. Ballads.   2. Tales.   3. Troubadour songs.   I. Title.
PN6110.B2L58   1996
398.27–dc20   96-10188
                                                                CIP

Printed in the United States of America

0 9 8 7 6 5 4 3 2 1

Fulcrum Publishing
350 Indiana Street, Suite 350
Golden, Colorado 80401-5093
(800) 992-2908 • (303) 277-1623

Acknowledgments

I wish to acknowledge the influences of people, stories, and music on my life. Thanks to the students at Stober Elementary School (including Emily Livo) who shared stories of music with me. Gratitude to my editor, Daniel Forrest-Bank, for his guidance and to Suzanne Barchers, Acquisitions Editor with Fulcrum Publishing, who as a former music teacher gave reactions and ideas that were quite pertinent. Finally, there is appreciation for the stories and music that are an important part of our world.

For three violinists who have enriched my life—my father David Jackson,
my brother Howard Jackson, and my granddaughter Jody Livo.

"In the fiddler's house, everyone dances."
—Itzhak Perlman

Contents

Troubadour's Storybag

"As long as the human spirit thrives on this planet, music in some living form will accompany and sustain it and give it expressive meaning."
—*Aaron Copland (1900–1990), American composer,*
from the London Times, *November 27, 1980*

Introduction

THE WORD "MUSIC" COMES from the Greek "muse." The Muses were nine Greek goddesses who presided over literature, the arts, and the sciences. The muse is the spirit thought to inspire an artist or poet, and is the source of genius or inspiration. In the Bible, Jubal was the father of all who play the harp and flute.

There are classical references to the "music of the spheres"—an ethereal music supposed by Pythagoras and other early mathematicians to be produced by the movements of the heavenly bodies. There also is the famous saying, "Music has charms to soothe a savage breast." One unknown muse said, "I wanted to remember the words, so I set them to music."

Music has been around forever. Early people believed that music was magic and could carry messages to the spirit world. Some people still believe that music carries all sorts of messages to our spirits. In Mexican folklore, there was a god who represented flowers, poetry, music, statesmanship, and the family. This god was carved in the form of a serpent with a bird's head and the scales of flowers.

Do you remember the fable of "The Blind Man and the Elephant"? In this fable, there were six blind men from Indostan who each felt a separate part of an elephant and each had a specific, personal idea of what an elephant was like. For instance, one of the blind men, after touching the elephant's ear, thought it was like a fan. All the blind men were partly right, but none experienced the entire creature. That fable is a good analogy of how each of us brings our own personal experiences to our understanding every day. Each person who experiences music has his or her own idea as to what music is, and what it does for all of us.

Several historical and general thoughts on the subject of music are appropriate here. Stone age hunters used a musical bow to hypnotize their prey. When an arrow was released from the bow, it created a humming sound. By adding strings of different lengths and thicknesses to the bow, it became a musical harp.

Ancient Athenians studied music as a discipline of mathematics, and during the medieval period, the trumpet was the coveted symbol of wealth and power and was outlawed for use by anyone except royalty and the upper Church hierarchy. When the Black Plague was at its height, the hurdy-gurdy was forbidden, because the plague seemed to follow the arrival of traveling minstrels. Removing the instrument was seen as a way of preventing the spread of the plague.

The original purpose of a ballad was to carry the news, to tell the stories of lovers, battles, people, history, and happenings. Because ballads are examples of good storytelling at its best—tersely told, stripped of all but the most significant details—a ballad has many implications for influencing our lives. Music, singing, playing, and dancing are part of the traditions of every culture.

Recent studies indicate that listening to music can increase one's I.Q. (especially Mozart's Sonata for Two Pianos), cows' milk production, and the growth of plants. As reported in the *Journal of the American Medical Association* in 1994, a study suggests that surgeons are likely to do a better job at the operating table with a little background music. Another study by scientists at Beth Israel Hospital in Boston reached the conclusion that musicians' brains are structured differently from other people's. In this study the researchers compared detailed brain scans of professional musicians and non-musicians. They concluded that some people are born with a magical sense of music, but without early training, the gift may be lost.

In education, a committee of twenty-five prominent Americans headed by David Rockefeller Jr., in the report titled "Coming to Our Senses" (*The Humanities in American Life*, University of California Press, Berkeley, 1980), cited a number of instances where innovative integration of arts instruction into school curricula stimulated children to higher achievement in traditional studies.

In research in brain development, researchers such as Drake University's Raymond Hock are suggesting children should have more creative experiences in schools, such as listening more to music and observing nature, as opposed to the emphasis on skills in the curricula.

As reported in newspapers and television, researchers at the University of California, Irvine, found that preschoolers who take music lessons may be on their way to doing better in math, chess, and even map-reading later on. Their ability to reason about how objects relate to each other was improved.

Therefore, what is more natural than melding music with stories about music and musical instruments? These tales can provide another experience with music that could expand our ideas and perceptions and enrich our understanding of the musical "elephant." Folklore sources are rich with explanations as to the origins of music and musical instruments.

We play music; dance, march, or move to music; sing with music; and tell stories with and about music. We even play games to music such as the standard musical chairs. Music has served to inspire participants in battle from the bagpipers in India to military bands at public ceremonies.

Stories

Why storytelling? Stories are light-as-air, deep-as-breath, transforming heirlooms passed down with beauty and form.

What is a story? It depends on who hears it. As listeners and readers, we all discover different things in the same story. Some things we are ready for, and we just skim the top off some stories. The same story can leave one person with a smile and another with tears. Whether we know it or not, we are all guided by voices of our ancestors—they had generations of memory in their heads. More about the ancient stories and oral history later.

Stories of events and peoples that are real, remembered, historical, or embellished are all part of us. There is none among us too old or too sophisticated to be touched by a story. As proof of this, consider Kassie S. Neou of the Cambodian Survivors Association, who was held prisoner by the Khmer Rouge, the Cambodian Communist party. At an address at the Denver Museum of Natural History, he remembered, "I was taken to jail in 1976 because I spoke three words of English. That was my crime. I survived execution just because guards wanted to keep me alive to tell them stories—Aesop stories."

What is the value of stories? Some say that stories make us more human. They help us live more lives than our own. Stories help us see the world from inside the skins of people different from ourselves. They help develop compassion and insight into the behavior of ourselves and others. A good story can show us the past in a way that helps us understand the present. One of the most important features of a story is that it develops the imagination. Stories also help us entertain ideas we never could have had without them. Stories are magical, particularly an oral story. They can take us out of ourselves and return us to ourselves; it is a self-transforming power.

Stories can be used to build self-confidence and persistence, to impart values and hopes, to demonstrate follies and triumphs, and to develop an optimistic outlook on life and show the listener or the reader that he or she is not the only one who ever had such experiences. There is no such thing as a story that is only a story.

Ancient stories are the best stories because they have been worked on over the ages by the "folk." The seemingly simple folk story is a combination of entertainment, history, astronomy, religion, literature, social and natural sciences, and imagination.

The ability to tell stories—by ancient peoples as well as today's suburbanites—is the only art that exists in all human cultures. It is through stories that we experience our lives. The ability to story is what sets people apart from all the other creatures of the earth. It may be the one element that defines us as humans.

With the advent of print, stories are now frozen in books. We no longer spend the long, dark winter nights telling one another stories. In fact, one opponent of too much television in our lives said that the light bulb—not television—destroyed storytelling. However it goes, we now learn most of our stories from books. For the purposes of this book, this is not bad. At least it gives us access to the stories that can help bring us imagination and joy. A great story is something that one cannot step into twice at the same place—somewhat like Heraclitus's river from mythology. That is the reason for the use of

4

stories in conjunction with music. We can find in stories something to build on for future experiences—different spots in the river.

Stories and Music

I have yet to be in a gathering of Finns when "Finlandia" is played where there are no quiet tears from some listeners. The music brings back so many memories and associations for the listener that emotions are rampant. The personal stories connected with the music give it much more emotional impact. If we know some stories of music, instruments, and musicians, we bring much more depth to our musical listening. Through tapes, radio, records, and live performances, we can have music with us wherever we go today to inspire, soothe, and entertain ourselves. Read or listen to these stories and then provide firsthand experiences with a favorite piece of music or instrument related to it. Combine the arts of storytelling and music—you will be surprised how far-reaching the results can be.

Bumper-sticker philosophy advertises: Art saves lives; Art is the part that makes us whole; The arts build community; Expose yourself to art! In a more serious way, the words of John Kennedy engraved at the Kennedy Center for the Performing Arts said, "Through the arts we will be remembered for our contributions to the human spirit." Therefore, listen, listen, listen; sing, sing, sing; and play, play, play! Experience story and music and create your own music! The muse is everywhere.

We get this story about the origins of music from a poem found in a sixteenth-century Nahua manuscript.

Where Music Came From
(Mexico)

LONG AGO, IN ANCIENT MEXICO, Tezcatlipoca (the sky god) and Quetzalcoatl (the wind god) noticed how quiet the world was. Every day sounded just like every other day—quiet! They discussed what they could do about this matter.

"Well, that is just the way it has always been on Earth," said Quetzalcoatl. "There has never been anything to hear. Why should there be?"

"I know that there can be something delightful to listen to," replied Tezcatlipoca. "As the sky god, I have heard amazing things around the Sun. Sun has something known as music everywhere. He is greedy, though, and refuses to share singing and music-making with anyone. He keeps it all to himself."

"Maybe we can do something about that," said Quetzalcoatl. "I don't know what we can do, but there must be something. Do you have any ideas?"

"You are the god of wind, so you should be able to bring music to the earth. You travel everywhere, why couldn't you go to where the Sun lives and capture music for us?" asked Tezcatlipoca.

"You are the sky god," answered Quetzalcoatl, "Why can't you do it?"

"Ah, dear friend, you are so fast you could sweep up the music in a hurricane and have it back here before Sun knows what has happened." After much discussion and debate on several improbable ideas, it always came back to the wind god stealing the music from Sun. Finally Quetzalcoatl agreed to go.

"Remember you first must land at the beach and find my three servants: Cane and Conch, Water Woman, and Water Monster. Order them to make you a bridge to where the Sun lives," advised the sky god, Tezcatlipoca.

Quetzalcoatl zoomed into the sky and flew until he had found the right beach. He did as he had been told and ordered the sky god's

6

servants to create a bridge. It was fantastic to watch them grab each other and stretch and grow and weave themselves into a colorful rope that made a bridge that reached out of sight into the sky.

The god of wind was uncertain, but he took a deep breath and blew winds that took him higher and higher and higher along the bridge into the sky. After a long time Quetzalcoatl came to where Sun lived. He noticed that as he got closer he heard the sounds of what must be music. It was like nothing he had ever heard before. It floated in the air—sometimes light, sometimes low, sometimes high, but always everywhere. He followed the sounds until he stood before the sun god himself. Quetzalcoatl saw that some of the sounds came from flutes, singers, and drummers.

The Sun recognized the wind god and ordered all the music to stop. Tezcatlipoca had followed Quetzalcoatl to make sure that he successfully captured music. When the Sun commanded the music to cease, Tezcatlipoca couldn't stand it. He roared, "Musicians, singers, players, come with us! You must come to Earth with us!"

What followed was a great storm of winds, thunder, lightning, and swirling darkness. Quetzalcoatl made noises that had never been heard before. It sent the musicians trembling, looking for a place to hide. Before they could hide, the gods of wind and sky snatched them up and flew back down the bridge to Earth.

The musicians soon saw that Earth was quite different from the place where Sun dwelled. There were creatures of every description, huge trees, birds that flew from tree to tree, and many colored flowers growing everywhere. There were also streams and lakes filled with all kinds of living things. The musicians gathered together and made music for the flowers that sang of their beauty and fragrance. They made music for the birds that flew to listen to this new sound.

Before long, the birds discovered they could make music of their own. Crickets started chirping. Jaguars added their own special sounds, while the tree toads joined in a chorus. Everywhere in the world there was music. Everything that lived on Earth discovered that it could add to the music and make it their own.

Before you could say, "That is how music came to the world," new sounds were discovered. These sounds filled the days and nights and brought great joy to everyone who heard them.

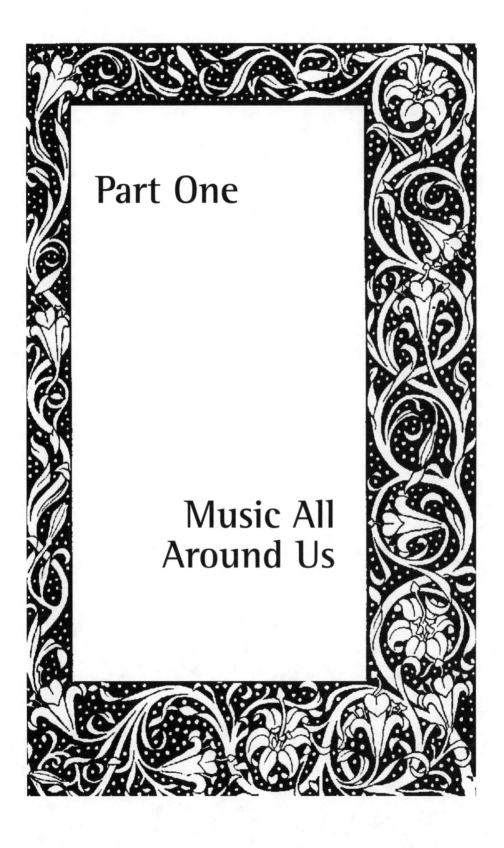

Part One

Music All Around Us

Old trickster Iktomi created a special songbag, but his music ends up to be rather sad.

Iktomi and His Bag of Songs

(United States)

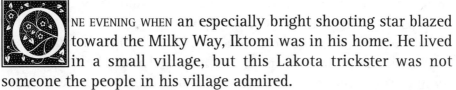NE EVENING WHEN an especially bright shooting star blazed toward the Milky Way, Iktomi was in his home. He lived in a small village, but this Lakota trickster was not someone the people in his village admired.

Iktomi was indifferent to affairs of the society and he avoided hunting, warfare, and other civic duties. He had a lazy, shiftless, easy life. Like con men of today, he preyed on his fellow people. In fact, his latest tricks had reduced him in the villagers' opinion to someone to be avoided at all costs. Being with Iktomi only meant trouble and problems.

Iktomi was not bothered by the fact that he had no friends and that people ignored him. He decided, however, that now would probably be a fine time to travel on and find new places and new faces on which to play his tricks. In those days, it was a Lakota custom that when a person set out on a journey, he was given gifts of foods and beads and a farewell party. However, there was none of that for the old trickster. No one was saddened by his leaving the village.

Iktomi gathered his few belongings and took off for new places and new adventures. He intended to go where people didn't know his mean tricks. He left on a particularly hot day filled with dust raised by wind gusts. After a few days, he found that he needed food and water. His stomach started growling and hurting from emptiness. Between the relentless sun and his hurting stomach, Iktomi felt sick, and he became unable to concentrate on his trip to somewhere. He staggered to the north and stumbled as he came to the rim of a high, rocky ridge. He was in despair and fear. Never had he been so hungry and thirsty and lonely.

And then, at the very top of the ridge, Iktomi looked down and saw stretched out before him a wonderful lush valley with a small meandering stream running down the middle. Around this stream swayed green grass, and every now and again rose a huge cottonwood tree. At first, Iktomi feared he only imagined this glorious sight. He closed his eyes and then slowly, fearfully, opened them, but the stream was still there. Iktomi could still see the water tumbling over rocks and winding through the valley.

Weak as Iktomi was, he found the strength to run and slide down the hillside as fast as he could to the stream. There he threw himself into the water. How it cooled him. He drew handfuls of water to gulp as he knelt in the water. He sipped and drank the fresh, cold water until he began to be reminded of how hungry he was.

Where was he to find food? Iktomi crawled to the edge of this wondrous stream and started to walk along it. Around one bend, he found a flock of ducks floating in the stream. Iktomi was so famished he almost threw himself into the water to grab at the ducks but decided that there had to be a better, surer way to get the ducks for his dinner.

Iktomi quietly oozed from the shore into the bushes behind him. He took a bag from his pack and pulled at the grasses on the shore. He stuffed these grasses into his bag until he had filled it. He stood up straight, threw the bag stuffed with grass over his shoulder and strolled back to the shoreline, making sure that the ducks would see him.

Yes indeed, the ducks did see him. They swam in circles as they looked at him and wondered what was in his bag. Finally, the curious ducks called to Iktomi, but he pretended not to hear them. The ducks started quacking and slapping the water with their wings. "What do you have in that bag?" they begged. "Tell us what it is."

Iktomi ignored them and continued to saunter along. "Why are you in such a hurry?" the ducks asked. As if he were quite impatient with them, Iktomi grudgingly told the ducks, "Keep your beaks out of my business. I have to get to the next village as quickly as I can."

The ducks asked, "Why?"

Again acting impatient, Iktomi answered, "Because! Don't you know there is going to be a special gathering and I am the singer for their dances? My songs are in this bag. It is my songbag of important music."

As he said this, Iktomi tapped his bag lovingly. He started to move on, and the ducks once more set up quacking and flapping. "Please stay. We want to dance. Sing us one of your songs and we will dance."

Iktomi pretended to be exasperated with the ducks. He fussed and he fumed at them, but after several more quacking and flapping bouts, he reluctantly agreed to sing for the ducks. He warned them that the first song he was going to sing was strictly for ceremonial dancing and that they had to be careful to follow his words. "This is the Shut-Eye Song. It means that you must dance with your eyes tightly closed and obey the words of the song. If you don't follow directions, bad things will happen to you."

The ducks swam to the shore and waddled up onto the sandy bank. They agreed to close their eyes as they danced.

Iktomi sang:

> Keep your eyes tightly closed,
> Dance to and fro with the song,
> With tightly closed eyes,
> Sway and dip and hop,
> Unclosed eyes will cause you grief,
> See the dance inside your eyelids.

The ducks kept time to the beat of the song and nearly all obeyed Iktomi and kept their eyes tightly shut. Iktomi knocked the first, fattest duck down with a stick, and never losing the rhythm of the song, he swung his stick again and again. One of the littlest of the ducks, though, had kept his eyes open and saw what was happening. "Open your eyes everyone," he cried. "Iktomi is knocking ducks on the head. He is trying to kill us all!"

In a flash, the rest of the ducks flew away. Their wings beat the air in a swishing, flashing flight. This didn't bother Iktomi, though. He had caught enough ducks to satisfy even his great hunger.

As Iktomi no longer needed his bag of songs, he opened it up and shook the grass out. Then he put the ducks he had knocked on the head in his bag. He went over to a large cottonwood tree and collected dry dead branches. He laid the branches out in a fire ring and built a fire. He dug a hole and buried the ducks in it. Then he covered the hole with hot coals and embers. This would be a wonderful batch of roast ducks indeed!

Iktomi sat with his back to the cottonwood tree, scrunched himself into a comfortable position, and took a nap while the smell of roasting ducks floated into the air. Then, out of nowhere, the wind picked up and blew the tree branches. The branches made funny sounds as they rubbed and banged against each other. This squeaking and snapping woke Iktomi up. He called up into the tree, "Old tree with dancing branches. Do not make such a noise. Dear branches, do not quarrel. Do not yell at each other. Shhh!" But the wind gusted wildly and the creaking and squeaking in the tree grew worse.

Iktomi climbed up into the tree to make peace among the branches. He called out to the waving branches, "Be calm. Do not attack each other." Just as Iktomi stuck his peacemaking hand between two quarreling branches, the wind stopped blowing. Iktomi's hand became wedged between two large branches. He was stuck hard and fast. To make matters worse, the wonderful smell of roasting ducks floated in the breeze past his twitching nose.

As Iktomi looked out over the countryside, he saw a fox trotting first one way, then another, in the distance. The fox's nose was to the ground and then in the air. He looked as if he was following something. Iktomi could see that the fox's ribs showed clearly. This was a hungry fox who ran and sniffed.

The fox didn't seem to be able to find a real trail. His efforts to find the delicious smell he sometimes smelled were as meandering as the stream. It looked as though the fox was tiring and was about to give up his search. What did Iktomi do, though? He was so frustrated at being caught in the tree that his brain went silly. Before he knew what he was doing, he was yelling at the fox, "Hey you! Don't come near here you mangy scavenger! Those ducks roasting in the ashes are mine. Don't even think of begging for a handout. Those ducks are mine, mine, mine, mine!"

The fox heard Iktomi. He stopped, sniffed the air, and said, "Ha! My nose didn't fool me." Between Iktomi's voice and the smell coming from the ducks, the fox found his way straight to the fire. The fox carefully dug at the smoldering ashes and snatched a juicy duck out of the hole. He tore the meat from the bones and ate it with lip-smacking gusto. He even cracked the bones and got the good marrow out of the middle of them. It seemed as if the fox was doing all of this in slow motion while Iktomi was caught in the tree with wisps of duck smoke rising to his nose. Iktomi began to drool and slobber from a combination of hunger and rage.

The fox didn't seem bothered by the saliva dropping from above. He looked up and said, "Why don't you come down and join me in this amazing feast of perfectly roasted ducks? As I never learned how to climb a tree, I can't bring any of these morsels up to you. You'll just have to get down here before the ducks cool." And then all Iktomi heard was the cracking and crunching of the duck bones.

As his stomach became full, the fox became full of love for his fellow beings. He decided that he would save one or two of the ducks for Iktomi. That would be only fair. Even as he thought this, though, he kept eating. No longer was he in an eating frenzy but was rather in a mellow, delicate eating mood. When the fox went back to the duck oven, he scattered the coals but couldn't find any more ducks. "What a careless glutton I have become. Oh, well, maybe Iktomi really isn't hungry," thought the fox. And then, with this newly filled stomach, the fox became droopy eyed and decided to take a nap. He stretched out on a nice bed of soft grasses and slept. When the fox awakened, he thanked Iktomi for being such a generous host. "When you have roast ducks again, don't forget to invite me," said the fox. He turned and trotted away.

Just as the fox was fading in the shimmering heat waves, another big gust of wind blew the branches open and Iktomi snatched his numb hand away. He climbed down the tree and ran to the duck pit. He lost all control and screamed and tore at his hair. He screeched insults at the fox, the tree, the ducks, and the world. It was a curious noise—his screeching while his stomach growled and rumbled—and all of it without a bag of music!

The following story explains why there are so many talented Gypsy musicians.

St. Peter and the Gypsies

(Yugoslavia)

ST. PETER WAS PREPARING for a trip to earth. God placed a fiddle on St. Peter's shoulders, but St. Peter didn't know this. He went into an inn where many people were having a good time. To his surprise, when the people saw the fiddle on his shoulders, they pleaded with him to play some music.

St. Peter did not know the fiddle was there, so the people who insisted that he play for them frightened him. He started to run away. The fiddle fell from his shoulders when he reached the door. St. Peter picked it up, then went straight to God.

"What does this mean, God? How did I get this fiddle?" he asked.

"That was an idea I had. I thought if you played music for people when they were together, it would keep them in a good humor," answered God. "Then they might not quarrel and fight with each other."

St. Peter thought about that for a while. "If what you say is true, maybe we need more musicians."

"Do you have any thoughts about who we could get to be musicians?" asked God.

"Let's create Gypsies," suggested St. Peter. "Let them make music and enchant people so that they won't fight and quarrel with each other when they gather."

"Let it be so," said God. And that is the way it has been ever since, and that is why there are so many talented Gypsy musicians throughout the world.

Today we are playing and experimenting with virtual reality games and experiences. This has been done before in story.

The Nightingale

(China)*

N CHINA, MANY YEARS AGO, there lived an emperor in a palace that was beautiful beyond belief. It was made entirely of fine porcelain, which was so fragile it had to be treated with extreme care.

The garden was full of extraordinary flowers. Some of them had little silver bells tied to them that tinkled perpetually, so no one could pass the flowers without taking the time to look at them. The whole garden was so big that even the gardener did not know where it ended.

Nearby there was a beautiful forest with giant trees and cool, deep lakes. The wood extended to the sea itself. Large ships sailing in the sea were able to sail right up under the branches of the trees. In these trees lived a nightingale. This nightingale sang songs so lovely that even a poor fisherman lay still to listen to it when he was drawing in his nets in the dark of the night.

The fisherman thought, "How beautiful it is." When he went back to work, though, he forgot about the nightingale's song. Each night he said the same thing when he heard the bird sing.

People from all over the world came to visit and admire the emperor's country. These travelers were impressed by the palace and the gardens, but when they heard the nightingale sing, they all said, "This is better than anything we have ever seen or heard." When these travelers returned to their homes, they described the song of the nightingale. Writers wrote many books about the emperor's town, his palace, and the garden, but they all praised the nightingale above everything else. Poets wrote books of poems about the nightingale and its songs. Artists painted impressive pictures of how they thought the nightingale looked. Of course some of these writings and pictures reached the emperor. He smiled as he read these books, sitting in his great golden chair. "What is this? The nightingale is the best of all?" he said. "I do not know anything about this nightingale. Is there such a thing in my kingdom?"

He asked his gentlemen-in-waiting, "Is there such a bird in my kingdom? Why have I never heard of it? Imagine my having to discover all of this from books?" To the grandest of all the gentlemen-in-waiting, the emperor said, "There is said to be a wonderful bird called a nightingale in my kingdom. People say that it is better than anything else in all my great estate. Why have I never been told about it?"

The grandest gentleman-in-waiting bowed and replied, "I have never heard the nightingale mentioned. It has never been presented in court. I do not know anything about it."

"I wish it to appear here this evening to sing to me," ordered the emperor. "It seems that everyone in the whole world knows what I possess but I know nothing of it!"

"Yes, my emperor. Even though I have never heard it mentioned before, I will seek the nightingale, and I will find it," replied the gentleman-in-waiting. Now there was the problem—where was he to find it? He ran throughout the palace, but no one he met in all of the rooms and corridors had ever heard of the nightingale.

He reported back to the emperor and said, "The nightingale must be a myth invented by those who wrote the books. Your Imperial Majesty must not believe everything that is written! Books are often mere inventions, written by people full of mischief."

"That cannot be," stormed the emperor. "The book in which I read about it was sent to me by the powerful emperor of Japan. It can't be untrue. I will hear this nightingale. I insist that it be here tonight. If it is not forthcoming, I will have the whole court trampled upon after supper."

The gentleman-in-waiting murmured, "Tsing-pe!" With that, he ran away again, up and down all the stairs, in and out all the rooms and corridors, slamming and banging all the doors. Half the court ran with him because none of them wished to be trampled.

At last they found a poor little maid in the kitchen who said, "Oh heavens! The nightingale? I know it very well. Yes indeed, it can sing. Every evening I am allowed to take broken meat to my poor sick mother who lives down by the shore. On my way back, when I am tired, I rest awhile in the wood, and then I hear the nightingale. Its song brings tears to my eyes. I feel as if my mother were kissing me."

"Oh, dear little kitchen maid," said the gentleman-in-waiting, "I will procure you a permanent position in the kitchen. I will grant you permission to see the emperor dining. I will do this if you will take us to the nightingale. The bird is commanded to appear at court tonight."

Half the court went out into the wood where the nightingale usually sang. As they were going along at their best pace, a cow began to low. "Oh," whispered a young courtier, "there we have it. What wonderful power for such a little creature. I have certainly heard it before."

The maid told him, "No, those are the cows lowing. We are still a long way from the place." Then frogs began to croak in the marsh.

"How beautiful!" exclaimed the Chinese chaplain. "It is just like the tinkling of church bells from the gentle winds."

"No, my esteemed chaplain, those are the frogs," explained the little kitchen maid. "I think we shall soon hear the nightingale, though."

And then, the nightingale began to sing. "Listen, listen! There it sits," said the little girl as she pointed to a little gray bird up among the branches.

"Is it possible?" asked the gentleman-in-waiting. "I should never have thought it was like that. How very common it looks. Maybe seeing so many grand people has frightened all its colors away."

"Little nightingale," called the little kitchen maid quite loud, "our gracious emperor wishes you to sing to him."

"With the greatest pleasure," said the nightingale, and it warbled away in a most delightful fashion.

The gentleman-in-waiting said, "It is just like crystal bells. Look at its little throat—see how it moves. It is extraordinary that we have never heard it before. I am sure the nightingale will be a great success at court."

The nightingale asked, "Shall I sing again for the emperor?" It mistakenly thought the emperor was present.

"My most precious little nightingale," said the gentleman-in-waiting, "I have the honor to invite your attendance at a court festival tonight. There you will charm His Gracious Majesty, the emperor, with your amazing singing."

"My singing sounds best among the trees," said the nightingale, but it went with them willingly when it heard that the emperor wished it.

The palace had been brightened up for this special event. The porcelain walls and floors shone by the light of many thousand golden lamps. The most beautiful flowers, all with tinkling bells, were arranged in the corridors. There was so much hurrying to and fro, that a great draft made the bells ring, filling the air with the tinkling. In the great reception room, a golden rod had been fixed so the nightingale would have a place to perch beside the emperor's golden chair.

The whole court was assembled, and the little kitchen maid had been permitted to stand behind the door—she now had the actual title of Cook. Everyone was dressed in their best finery. Their eyes were turned toward the little gray bird. The emperor nodded at it.

The nightingale sang its delightful song. The song brought tears into the emperor's eyes, then the tears rolled down his cheeks. The nightingale sang more beautifully than ever and its notes melted the hearts of all the listeners. The emperor was so charmed that he said the nightingale should have his golden slipper to wear round its neck. The nightingale declined with thanks—it had already been sufficiently rewarded.

"I have seen tears in the eyes of the emperor," said the nightingale. "That is my richest reward. The tears of an emperor have a wonderful power." With this, the bird burst again into its sweet, heavenly song.

The ladies of the court thought, "That is the most delightful coquetting we have heard." They took water into their mouths to try to imitate the sounds of the bird. They thought their gurgling was equal to the nightingale. But they were greatly mistaken.

The nightingale had pleased everyone, even the lackeys and the chambermaids. That was quite an accomplishment as everyone knew they were the most difficult people to please.

Yes indeed, the little gray nightingale had made a sensation. It was to stay at court and have its own cage. It also had the liberty to walk out twice a day and once in the night. However, it always had twelve footmen. Each footman held a ribbon tied around the nightingale's leg. There was not much pleasure in an outing of that sort.

Everyone in the town talked about the marvelous bird. When two people met, if one said to the other, "Night," the other answered, "Gale." Then they would sigh with perfect understanding. Eleven cheesemongers' children were named after the bird, but not one of them could sing a note.

One day a large package came for the emperor. Outside was written the word "Nightingale."

The emperor said, "Here we have another new book about our celebrated bird." But it was not a book. It was a little work of art in a box. It was an artificial nightingale exactly like the living one except that it was studded all over with sparkling diamonds, rubies, and sapphires.

When the artificial bird was wound up, it would wag its tail and sing one of the songs the real nightingale sang. The tail glittered with silver and gold. On a ribbon tied around its neck was a message, "The emperor of Japan's nightingale is very poor compared to the emperor of China's."

Everyone who saw it said, "Oh, how beautiful!" The messenger who brought the artificial bird was immediately named The Imperial Nightingale-Carrier-in-Chief.

Someone said, "Now they must sing together. What a duet that will be!" It was decided that the two birds had to sing together. They did not get on very well, though, for the real nightingale sang in its own way, but the artificial one could only sing waltzes.

"There is no fault in that," said the music master. "The artificial bird sings perfectly in time and correct in every way." Then the artificial bird had to sing alone. It was just as great a success as the real nightingale had been, and it was much prettier. It glistened like bracelets and breastpins with its jewels, silver, and gold.

The artificial bird sang the same tune three and thirty times over, and yet it was not tired. People would have happily heard the tune from the beginning again, but the emperor said that the real bird must have its turn now. But where was it? It had flown out of the open window, back to its own green woods, but no one had noticed it going.

"What is the meaning of this?" demanded the emperor.

All of the courtiers complained and said that the nightingale was a most ungrateful bird. "We have got the best bird though," they said. They had the artificial bird sing again. This was the thirty-fourth time that they had heard the same tune, but they did not know it thoroughly even yet because it was so difficult.

The music master praised the artificial bird tremendously and insisted that it was better than the real nightingale, "Not only is it prettier with all of its jewels, but it sings better, too.

"You see Your Imperial Majesty and ladies and gentlemen, with the real nightingale, you never know what you will hear. With the artificial one, everything is decided beforehand. So it is, and so it must remain. It can't be otherwise. You can account for things. You can open the bird up and see the human ingenuity in arranging how the waltzes go, and how one note follows upon another."

"Those are exactly my thoughts," everyone said, and with this, the music master received permission to show the bird to the public the very next Sunday. They were also to hear it sing, said the emperor. So the public all heard the artificial bird and became as enthusiastic over it as if they had drunk themselves merry on tea, because of course, that is a thoroughly Chinese habit.

They all said, "Oh!" and stuck their forefingers in the air and nodded their heads. But the poor fisherman who had heard the real nightingale said, "It certainly sounds very nice, and it is very nearly like the real one, but there is something wanting. I don't know what."

The real nightingale was banished from the kingdom. The artificial bird had its place on a silken cushion, close to the emperor's bed. All the presents it received of gold and precious jewels were scattered around it. Its title was Chief Imperial Singer-of-the-Bed-Chamber. In rank it stood first on the emperor's left side, for the emperor reasoned that the seat nearest his heart was the most important one. After all, even an emperor's heart is on the left side!

The music master wrote five and twenty volumes about the artificial bird. The treatise was very long and was written in all the most difficult Chinese characters. Everybody said they had read and understood it, for otherwise they would have been reckoned stupid, and then their bodies would have been trampled upon.

Things went on in this way for a whole year. The emperor, the court, and all the other Chinese knew every little gurgle in the song of the artificial bird by heart. In fact, they liked it all the better for this. They could all join in the song themselves. Even the street boys sang, "Zizizi! cluck, cluck, cluck!" The emperor sang it too.

One evening when the bird was singing its best and the emperor was lying in bed listening to it, something gave way inside the bird with a "whizz." "Whirr!" went all the wheels, and then the music stopped. The emperor jumped out of bed and sent for his private physicians, but what good could they do?

They sent for the watchmaker, who after a good deal of talk and examination got the works to go again somehow. He said the artificial bird would have to be spared as much as possible because it was so worn out. He also told them he could not renew the works so as to be sure of the tune. This was a great blow!

They now dared to let the artificial bird sing only once a year, and hardly that. The music master made a little speech using all the most difficult Chinese words. He said the bird was just as good as ever, and his saying it made it so.

Five years passed, then a great grief came upon the nation. The people were all very fond of their emperor, but now he was ill and could not live, or so it was said. A new emperor was already chosen, and people stood about in the street and asked the grandest gentleman-in-waiting how the emperor was getting on. He just shook his head.

The emperor lay pale and cold in his gorgeous bed. The courtiers thought he was dead, so they all went off to pay their respect to their new emperor. The lackeys ran off to talk matters over, while the chambermaids gave a great coffee party. Cloth had been laid down in all the rooms and corridors to muffle the sounds of footsteps, so it was very, very quiet.

But the emperor was not dead yet. He lay stiff and pale in his gorgeous bed with velvet hangings and heavy golden tassels. There was an open window high above him and the light of the moon streamed in upon the emperor and the artificial bird beside him.

The poor emperor could hardly breathe. He seemed to have a great weight on his chest. He opened his eyes and saw Death sitting on his chest wearing the emperor's own golden crown. In one hand Death held the emperor's golden sword, and in the other his imperial banner. From among the folds of the velvet hangings many curious faces peered at the emperor. Some were hideous, others gentle and pleasant. They were all the emperor's good and bad deeds, which now looked him in the face while Death was weighing him down.

"Do you remember that?" whispered one after the other. "Do you remember this?" They told him so many things that the perspiration poured down his face.

"I never knew that," said the emperor. "Music, music! Sound the great Chinese drums," he cried, "that I may not hear what they are saying." But they went on and on, and Death sat nodding his head at everything that was said. "Music, music!" shrieked the emperor. "You precious little golden bird, sing, sing! I have loaded you with precious stones and even hung my own golden slipper around your neck. Sing, I tell you, sing!"

The bird stood silent. There was nobody to wind it up, so of course, it could not go. Death continued to fix the great empty sockets of its eyes upon the emperor, and all was silent, terribly silent.

Suddenly, close to the window, there was a burst of lovely song. It was the living nightingale, perched on a tree branch outside. It had heard of the emperor's need and had come to bring him comfort and hope. As the nightingale sang, the faces around the emperor became fainter and fainter, and the blood coursed with fresh vigor in his veins and through his feeble limbs. Even Death himself listened to the song and said, "Go on, little nightingale, go on!"

"Yes, if you will give me the gorgeous golden sword. Yes, if you will give me the imperial banner. Yes, if you will give me the emperor's crown."

Death gave back each of these treasures for a song, and the nightingale went on singing. It sang about a quiet churchyard where roses bloom, where elder flowers scent the air, and where the fresh grass is ever moistened anew by the tears of mourners. This song brought to Death a longing for his own garden, and like a cold gray mist he passed out of the window.

"Thank you, thank you!" cried the emperor. "You heavenly little bird, I know you. I banished you from my kingdom, and yet you have charmed the evil visions away from my bed by your song and even kept Death away from my heart. How can I ever repay you?"

"You have rewarded me," said the nightingale. "I brought tears to your eyes the very first time I ever sang to you, and I shall never forget it. Those are the jewels that gladden the heart of a singer. But sleep now and wake up fresh and strong. I will sing to you."

The nightingale sang again and the emperor fell into a sweet, refreshing sleep. The sun shone in his window and he awoke refreshed and well. None of his attendants had yet come back to him for they thought he was dead. Only the little nightingale was there, singing.

"You must always stay with me," begged the emperor. "You shall sing only when you like, and I will break the artificial bird into a thousand pieces."

"Don't do that," said the nightingale. "It did all the good it could. Keep it as you have always done. I can't build my nest and live in the palace. Just let me come whenever I like. Then I will sit on the branch in the evening and sing to you. I will sing to cheer you and to make you thoughtful, too. I will sing to you of happy people and of those that suffer. I will sing about the good and the evil kept hidden from you. The little singing bird flies far and wide to the poor fisherman and to the peasant's home. It flies to many people who are far from you and your court. I love your heart more than your crown, and yet there is an odor of sanctity around the crown, too. I will come and I will sing to you. However, you must promise me one thing."

"Everything and anything!" said the emperor, who stood there in the imperial robes that he had just put on. He held the sword heavy with gold upon his heart.

"Only one thing I ask you. Tell no one that you have a little bird who tells you everything. It will be better so."

Then the nightingale flew away. The attendants came in to look after their dead emperor—and there he stood—bidding them "Good morning!"

*An original literary tale by Hans Christian Andersen.

When a king eavesdrops, it sets the story in motion for intrigue and a successful quest for amazing objects. This story of treasures "fit for a king" can be compared to the story of "The Nightingale."

The Talking Bird and the Singing Tree

(Russia)

ANY, MANY YEARS AGO in Russia, there was a very curious king who eavesdropped on his subjects from his windows. A rich merchant and his three daughters lived in the king's city. One day, the king overheard these three maidens talking with their father. The oldest daughter told her father, "I wish I were married to the king's caterer! He is my heart's delight."

The middle daughter laughed and said, "If only the king's body servant would notice me and take me for his bride."

The youngest daughter drew herself up straight and tall, tossed her head so her hair flowed behind, and said, "I should like to be married to the king himself. If I were his wife, I would give him two sons and one daughter."

Her sisters scorned her ambition. How dare she think she was worthy to be the wife of the king?

The king thought about this for some time and then he fulfilled all of their wishes. He married the eldest daughter to his caterer, the middle daughter to his body servant, and took the youngest to wife himself. She indeed was lovely enough to be the wife of a king.

The king lived quite happily with his young wife until she became pregnant. When her time to give birth came and she was having labor pains, the king wanted to send for the best midwife of his city. The king's sisters-in-law said, "Why send for a midwife? We ourselves can do what needs to be done. How hard is it to help a baby be born?"

The queen gave birth to a handsome son, but her sisters told the king that his wife had given birth to a puppy. They put the newborn baby in a box and dropped it in the pond in the middle of the king's garden.

26

The king was furious with his wife and wanted to have her shot. As luck would have it, some visiting kings talked him out of this, arguing that a first offense should be forgiven. So the king forgave her and postponed punishment in case such a thing should happen a second time.

One year later, the queen gave birth to another handsome son. This time her sisters told the king that it was another unusual baby—it was a kitten. The king became even more enraged and wanted to put his wife to death immediately. People in his court pleaded for mercy and talked him out of it again, so he postponed punishment. He promised that there would be no mercy if it should happen a third time.

The sisters put the second baby into a box, and just as they had done before, they dropped it into the pond in the middle of the king's garden.

The queen became pregnant for a third time and bore a beautiful daughter. The sisters told the king that his wife had once again given birth to a very unusual baby. The furious king ordered a gallows to be erected to hang his wife. As luck would have it, some kings from other countries were visiting and they convinced him, "Rather, build a chapel next to the church and put your wife in it. Then whoever goes to mass will spit in her face."

The king followed this advice. People not only spat in the poor queen's face but they also hurled whatever they had in their hands at her. It could be a moldy loaf of bread or sticky cakes. They didn't care. They just hurled it at her.

As for the queen's three babies that had been dropped into the pond in the middle of the king's garden, the king's gardener had found them and taken them to his childless wife. They brought them up with love and tenderness.

It seems that this gardener did not just grow excellent plants. These children of the king grew not by the year, but by the month—not by the day, but by the hour. The princes became handsome youths such as no mind can imagine nor words describe. The princess was such a beauty that she took one's breath away! When they were of age, they asked the gardener to allow them to build a house outside the town.

The gardener and his wife gave them their permission, and they built a fine big home and lived in it happily. The brothers delighted in catching hares. One day they went hunting and the sister remained at home alone. A little old woman came to the house and told the maiden, "Your house is beautiful and appealing, but you lack three things."

"What do we lack?" asked the princess. "It seems to me that we have everything we need."

The old woman replied, "You lack the talking bird, the singing tree, and the water of life."

The brothers returned from the hunt and the sister went out to greet them. "My brothers, I have been told that we have everything except three things."

"What do you not have, little sister?" asked her brothers.

"We do not have the talking bird, the singing tree, or the water of life," she told them.

The elder brother begged her, "Little sister, trust in me. I will go forth and get these marvels for you. I will thrust this penknife into the wall. If I die or am killed, blood will begin to drip from the knife, and you will know that I am dead."

With that, he left. He walked for a long time and came to a forest. A little old man sat on a tree, and the prince asked him, "Do you know how I can get the talking bird, the singing tree, and the water of life?"

The man gave the prince a little spool and said, "Follow this spool wherever it rolls." The spool began to roll and the prince followed it. It rolled up to a high mountain and vanished from sight. The prince started to climb up the mountain. He was halfway to the top and then he suddenly vanished too.

At his house, blood started to drip immediately from his penknife and the sister said to the younger brother, "Our brother must surely have died."

"I will go little sister. I will find the talking bird, the singing tree, and the water of life."

The sister packed him some food for his journey. He left. He walked for a very long time and then he came to a forest. A little old man was sitting on a tree. The prince asked him, "Little grandfather, how can I get the talking bird, the singing tree, and the water of life?"

The little old man told him, "Here is a spool. Follow it wherever it rolls." The man threw the spool and it began to roll. The prince followed it. It rolled up to a high mountain and vanished from sight. The prince started climbing the mountain. He reached the halfway point and poof! He suddenly vanished too.

Back at their home, the sister waited for him many, many years, but he did not come back. "My second brother must have died too," she thought. "I'll find the talking bird, the singing tree, and the water of life."

She set out the next day. She walked for some time, a short time or a long time, and came to a forest. On a tree there sat a little old man. "Little grandfather, how can I get the talking bird, the singing tree, and the water of life?" she asked him.

"You cannot get them! Much cleverer people than you have tried, but they all perished," he told her.

"Please tell me," she begged.

"Here is a spool. Follow it," he said as he gave her a spool.

After some time, a short time or a long time, this spool rolled up to a high mountain. As the sister began to climb, she heard voices shouting to her. "Where are you going? We shall kill you! We shall devour you!" But she kept on climbing and climbing. She came to the top of the mountain, and there sat the talking bird.

"Can you tell me where I can find the singing tree and the water of life?" she asked the bird.

"Go over there," the bird said. "You will find the singing tree."

The sister took the talking bird with her and followed the sounds of much music until she came to the singing tree. There were all kinds of birds singing in this tree. She broke off a branch with its birds and took it with her.

The sister went on until she came to the water of life. She gathered a pitcher of it to take home. She began to climb down the mountain, sprinkling the water of life on the ground as she walked.

Suddenly her brothers jumped up and said, "Ah, little sister. We have been asleep a long time."

"Yes, dear brothers. If it were not for me you would have slept here forever," she said. "I have the talking bird, the singing tree, and the water of life."

The brothers were filled with joy. The three of them went home and planted the singing tree in their garden. It grew and spread its branches out over the whole garden, and birds sang in it in a variety of voices.

One day the brothers went hunting their favorite animal, hares. They happened to meet the king out in the woods. He liked these hunters and asked them to come to see him. "We shall ask our sister's permission. If she grants it, we shall certainly come."

The brothers returned from the hunt. Their sister met them and greeted them joyfully. "Give us permission, little sister, to visit the king. We met him while we were hunting, and he very graciously invited us to come."

The princess gave them her permission, and they went to visit the king. The king received them cordially and invited them to a great feast. As they visited with him, the brothers invited the king to visit them in turn.

Sometime later, the king came to call on them, and the brothers and sister greeted him with joy and hospitality. What an honor! They showed him the singing tree and the talking bird. The tree and bird amazed the king. "Here I am, the king, and I do not have anything this wonderful!" he exclaimed.

Then the sister and the brothers told the king, "We have found out that we are your children." The king learned the whole truth and was overjoyed. He freed the queen from the chapel, and they all lived together for many years in great happiness and beauty, enjoying the talking bird and the singing tree.

In this Irish folktale, the king's son finds a very special singing bird and along with it, his future.

The Bird Singing in the Middle of the Woods

(Ireland)

NCE UPON A TIME when magic was everywhere, there was a king, his wife, and their son. They were a very happy royal family and they ruled wisely. Tragedy struck, though, and the queen became sick and died. The king missed her, but he saw how much his son missed having a mother, so he started thinking about marrying again.

In a kingdom nearby dwelled a queen who was a widow. She had three young sons about the same age as the king's son. The more the king thought about it, the more he thought it would be good if he and the queen married. Then their sons would have both a mother and a father. His son would also have other youngsters to play with. Not only that, the king and queen could combine their two smaller kingdoms into one grand kingdom.

The king courted the queen, and she was eager to marry him. The wedding was grand and full of joy for everyone. The king treated the queen's sons just as if they were his own. The queen, however, was a bitter, mean woman and she was always favoring her sons over the king's. In fact, she plotted to turn the king against his own son.

The king had a magnificent stallion in his stable. This horse was his favorite of all the horses, even to the point that when his own son asked to ride him as he often did, the king said, "That horse is too valuable to take any chances with. Someday you will be able to ride him. Until then, no."

The queen made up stories about the king's son. She told him, "Your son often takes that horse out of the stable. He doesn't listen to you at all."

Then the queen's three sons thought they would show the king, so they took the fine horse out of the stable and drove it over a cliff. The queen said, "See, I told you your son didn't obey you about that horse. Now, see what he has done."

Of course, the king's son denied it, but the king didn't know whom to believe. A short while after that, the four sons were out hunting together, and the king's son got separated from the others. "Let's fix him," plotted the queen's sons. "Let's kill the king's best greyhound." They stuck the dog with their swords and killed it.

When they came back to the castle, the dog was missed. The king asked, "Where is that favorite dog of mine?" Everyone searched all over the castle but there was no dog. The queen and her sons said, "Your son took the hound out this morning."

Later, the dog was found dead, and the king's son got the blame for killing it. "I will have to banish you from this kingdom," the king sadly told his son. The queen was delighted when she heard this. Just then, a neighboring gentleman rode into the castle courtyard and gave the true story to the king.

"I saw it all happen," he said, "as I was passing through the woods. If you look at your son's hunting clothes, there should be no blood on them. I hazard a guess, though, that there will be blood on the other boys' clothes."

The king sent for the clothes and sure enough! It was just as the neighbor said. The king was bewildered and called the boys to him. "You are not to go out hunting again unless I am with you."

"I will be sure to keep my eyes open," he said to himself. "I'll see whatever there is to be seen."

They all went hunting the next week. As they rode into the woods, the king was watching all the time. "How can I put our sons to the test?" he thought as he rode.

They came to the very middle of the woods and heard a bird start to sing. Never in all the world had another bird sung like that. The song was sweet, pure, and full of music. The king loved music and thought he could listen to that bird forever. "If I had that bird singing to me every day in my castle I would live long and die happy," he thought.

Then it came to him that he could get the bird and test the boys at the same time. He called them around him. "Do you hear that singing

32

bird? Well, whichever one of you will bring that bird to me alive and singing will get half of my kingdom now and the rest of it after I am dead."

The four boys took off to capture the bird. The bird flew from tree to tree, singing its sweet song the whole time. After a while, it flew into a hole in a pile of rocks. The four boys moved rocks and searched for the bird. At last they came to a rock they could not move. They cut down a tree and using it as a lever, they managed to move the rock slowly.

They found a big, deep hole like a well where the rock had been. It went down, down, down. One of the boys threw a small stone down the hole and they heard it land and bounce a long ways down. They got a long rope to use to go down the hole. They drew lots to see who would go down to follow the bird. The first lot fell to the eldest son of the queen. The other three boys lowered him down the hole on the rope. It was very dark in the hole and it wasn't too long until they heard the eldest son shouting and bawling to be pulled up.

When the other boys got him back up, he told them there was a man with a spear trying to stick him when he got down to the bottom of the hole. They drew lots again and this time the lot fell to the second son of the queen, but he did no better. He had hardly landed on the bottom when he started to yell for them to pull him up. "The man with the spear was waiting to stick me," he gasped.

The queen's third son suffered the same fate. Finally, it was the king's son's turn to go down. He didn't waste any time. As soon as his feet touched the bottom, he made a lunge at the man with the spear to grapple with him. But the man with the spear only laughed. "I am here to test the courage of anyone that comes down." He continued, "You are the first man who has had the courage to face me. As you are here, maybe I can lead you to where you are going."

The king's son told him the whole story of the singing bird and how he was trying to capture it for his father.

"The bird you seek lives in a castle a few miles away, with her father. There is only one thing to remember—when you come to that castle, you'll be offered gracious hospitality with food and drink. You must not eat a bite or drink a sip inside the walls of that castle. I will also loan you my horse. He will be of great help to you, but remember, be very careful with my horse." With that the man handed the horse over to the king's son.

The king's son thanked him most politely and rode away to the castle under the earth. He was given a great welcome there. His horse was put in the stable with food and water. Next, they spread a table with all kinds of delicious food and drink for him. But he remembered the words of the man with the spear and refused to taste or drink any of it. He did tell the underground king of the singing bird and his search for it.

"You are not the first to come in search of the bird," the underground king said. "The singing bird is really my daughter. However, you may not be the last to search for her, either. First, you must pass a test. The man who passes this test can marry my daughter. Here is the test. You will hide for three days. I will search for you. If I do not find you, I will hide for three days, and you must look for me. If I find you, or if you fail to find me, you will die. If I don't find you, but you find me, you may marry my daughter."

"I accept your test," agreed the king's son. He went out to the stable to check on his horse and make sure that everything was well with it. Imagine his surprise when the horse spoke to him, "Tomorrow the king and his soldiers will pull the place apart looking for you. You won't be able to escape them unless you follow my directions. Pull one hair out of my tail and go yourself into its place. The minute you do this, you will take the shape of a hair of my tail."

The next morning, when he was supposed to hide, the king's son did as the horse had instructed him. The king and his men searched high and low but could find no sign of him. In the evening, the young man was back in his right shape again. "You escaped today, but you will not escape me a second time," the underground king promised.

The king's son went out to tend to the horse, and again, the horse spoke to him, "You escaped today, but it might not work a second time. Tomorrow, pull a tooth out of my lower jaw and go into the place of the tooth."

The next morning, the king's son did as the horse had told him. The underground king searched for him all day but couldn't find any trace of the king's son. That evening, the king said, "You escaped today, but you surely will not escape a third time."

Later in the evening when the son went out to check on the horse, it told him, "Pull a nail out of one of my horseshoes and go into the hole in its place."

Again, the king failed to find the hidden son. "You bested me these past three days," the king said. "But you can be mighty certain that you won't find me when I hide. Then you will pay for all the trouble you have caused me."

In the morning, the king went off to hide and the son searched high and low without finding a trace of the king. He stopped out in the stables with his heart in his boots and held the horse's head. As he petted it, he told it his story of failure.

"Go to the orchard," said the horse, "to the tree that is the farthest from the castle gate. Pick the apple that is the nearest to the back wall of the orchard. Get your knife and go to cut it."

The king's son did as the horse had told him. Just as he was about to cut the apple ... "Hold your knife!" shouted the underground king, who was hiding in the apple. "You have me today but it will be a much different day tomorrow!"

The next morning, the king again went to hide. The son went straight out to the stable to the horse, and the horse said, "Go to the castle and get the loan of a gun. Then go down to the lake and aim at the biggest drake swimming with the ducks."

The king's son did as he had been told. Sure enough, the underground king was hiding in the shape of a duck. "You have me again," roared the king. "No matter how good you are, though, I'll beat you tomorrow, and then you will die a terrible death."

For the third time, the king went to hide, and the young man went to the stable for his instructions. "Be in no hurry today," said the horse. "Spend the day getting to know the daughter. That won't be hard to do, because she is a fine, lovely girl. Persuade her to take you out for a walk. Make sure the walk lasts all day and that you look at all her father's fine lands and visit her friends all around the place. When you come home in the evening, sit with her in front of the fireplace. When you get the chance, take the enchanted ring off her finger and pretend to throw it into the fire."

The horse was right. The day went quickly, and the daughter was delightful. That evening they were sitting in front of the fire. It was warm and cozy there. As they talked, the king's son found a chance to slip the ring off her finger and was motioning to throw it into the fire when … "Hold your hand!" ordered the king as he came out of his hiding place. He had been hiding under one of the sparkling jewels in the ring. "This is an enchanted ring," said the king, "and it is by its magic that my daughter is able to take the shape of a singing bird. It was because of the magic that my daughter saw you in the woods and led you here to my country under the ground. I had to test you because many are the men that have come looking for my daughter's hand in marriage, and only the best of men is good enough for my daughter. You have passed the test, and now you can marry her."

They were married the very next morning. They were quite happy. After a while, the young man told his wife and her father about what was happening in his own kingdom and how his stepmother was trying to turn his father against him. The three of them set out for the young man's country and explained everything to the son's father. They explained the magic of the singing bird and their country underground. "The queen was the cause of all the troubles," the son explained. By this time, the king knew his son was right, so the queen and her sons were sent back to her castle and given strict orders to stay there.

The king's son and his wife spent half of the year in his country and half of the year in her country. When they were with the son's father, the wife sometimes treated him to her singing. "I knew that anything that could make such wonderful music was magical," said the king.

When the two kings died, the son and his wife ruled with wisdom and joy over both countries.

Suggestions for Extending Experiences

♪ Iktomi had a bag of songs. What favorite songs would you keep in a songbag?

♪ Share *ABC: Musical Instruments from the Metropolitan Museum of Art* (New York: Harry N. Abrams, 1982). Notice the range of complexity of the instruments, from the *quena,* a Peruvian flute made of metal and fabric, to the harpsichord. Visit a crafter of musical instruments (call a musical instrument store for names of local instrument makers). How did this person get started making instruments? What is his or her favorite instrument? Why?

♪ Tape a folk story or folk song in a natural setting with real sound effects. For example, in the spring when frogs are singing, read and tape "Froggie Went A-Counting" with frogs in the background. If the frogs stop singing when you read, tape the frogs and use the tape as background music at a later time. Other stories to read with frog accompaniment include Vivian French's *A Song for Little Toad* (Cambridge, MA: Candlewick Press, 1995) or Denise Fleming's *In the Small, Small Pond* (New York: Henry Holt, 1993).

♪ Go on a listening trip to observe the music of nature. Sit by a stream, listen to crickets, identify different bird songs, or write a poem about the sounds of the wind.

♪ Go on a nature walk to find nature instruments. Use seed pods as shakers. Use sticks as percussive instruments. Blow on a leaf between your lips. Make reeds into whistles. You can also grow gourds and let them dry several months. The seeds will rattle inside, making shakers.

♪ Develop a resource bibliography of books related to making instruments.

♪ The *palos de agua* or "rain stick" is an instrument used to imitate the sounds of rain. Rain sticks originated in northern Chile, and it is said the Diaguita Indians used them in ceremonies to call on the spirits of rain. Make your own rain stick with a mailing tube, nails, and pebbles. Hammer the nails into the tube in a spiral pattern. Insert the pebbles, and seal both ends. Decorate your rain stick.

♪ Create a poster related to one of the stories in this section.

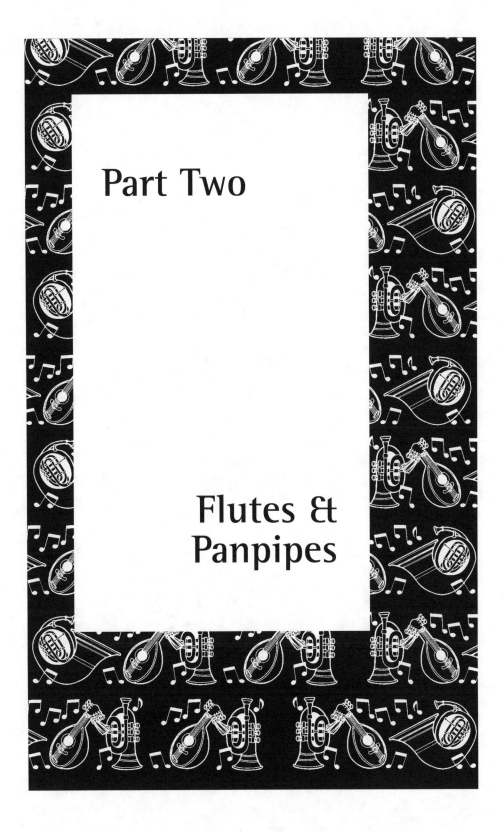

Part Two

Flutes &
Panpipes

This story was told to me by Charles Eagle Plume, who granted permission for me to use it here.

The Gift of the Elk

(United States)

 YOUNG WARRIOR with long braided hair loved a special young girl. He was a poor orphan youth without family or a lodge of his own.

One morning, he met her at the watering-place and told her of his love for her. She just laughed at him and said, "Who do you think you are? Why should I marry someone who lives among the tents without a home?" She went on to insult and revile him. "I am the daughter of the chief and who are you?" Her manner toward him was haughty and arrogant.

The rejected fellow was full of shame. "It would be just as well if I died now. There is nothing for me here in this village," he thought.

At dawn, the warrior shot an arrow northward and walked after it. He walked until evening and was just about to stop and rest when he discovered a fat deer impaled by his arrow. He cut it up and roasted a piece of the meat. After he had eaten, the hurt in his heart eased, and because he was tired, he soon fell asleep beside the fire.

It went like that for four days. The young warrior would shoot an arrow at dawn, find a deer killed by the arrow in the evening, butcher the animal, cook the meat, and eat it each day. Finally, he felt a little more cheerful.

On the fourth evening, as he sat alone by the fire, the boy thought, "I might as well go back home to the village." Then a strange sound came to him from a grove of trees. He thought he heard human voices. Expecting the worst, he thought, "What if they do kill me? There is nothing left for me. In fact, didn't I come this way seeking death?"

41

The voices drew nearer and he recognized the language they were speaking. "They are speaking Sioux," he thought. There were two voices. One of them said, "Friend, you give it to him," but then the other voice replied, "No, friend, you give it to him." The first voice spoke again, "Friend, you tell him properly." Again, the other speaker refused, "But no, friend, you tell him." At last the two speakers stopped just within the circle of firelight, and the boy saw an amazing thing. They were the handsomest young men he had ever seen. As they stood there in front of him, their bodies seemed to emit a glimmering and glowing light.

After a long silence, one spoke, "Boy, we know that you have much pain in your heart, but this will never be so a second time. Listen closely." They had with them a long flute and one of them began to play. The youth heard a sweet piercing sound come from the flute. The one playing it held it out to the boy. "Take this with you and go home. At midnight when the people are sleeping, walk through the camp playing this flute, and you will find that all the women will get up and follow you." The two handsome men turned around, and before the astonished youth's eyes, he saw two elk disappear among the trees.

The boy returned home to his village. It was late when he got there and everyone was asleep. He walked among the tents playing the flute. As the music filled the air, the women all got up from their beds and began to follow him, dragging their blankets behind them. They crowded around him, but he ignored them all. He was enchanted by the wonderful music he was playing.

From among the women one slender young maiden stepped out in front of him and repeatedly asked him, "Don't you remember me? I am the chief's daughter." But strangely the young man only heard the sound of the wonderful music that came from the mouth of the flute.

One girl didn't join the throng of women and was sitting alone quietly in her lodge. It was she that the youth sought out and married.

It is said that this is the story of the gift of the courting flute.

Who was the god of nature and shepherds? What did he look like? What were his habits? What did he have to do with music?

The Pipes of Pan
(Greece)

N ANCIENT TIMES, when the world was filled with gods, goddesses, and various spirits, Pan, the Greek god of nature and shepherds, had one major preoccupation—chasing the nymphs (beautiful maidens who were lesser divinities of nature).

Pan resembled a goat. He had a pointed beard, shaggy legs, and cloven feet. He had a turned-up nose, goat ears, and goat horns. He gleefully chased every nymph he saw. That wasn't enough, so sometimes he would dive into the river to swim after naiads (spirits of the lakes, rivers, and fountains who derived their life from the water in which they dwelled and in return gave life to the water). He searched throughout the groves for dryads (nymphs whose lives were bound up with that of a tree and who perished when the tree died or was destroyed).

Pan loved noise and riot, and yet he also liked lonely places in the mountains and hills. His anger was terrible, and he could give people horrible nightmares. Pan dwelt in forests and was dreaded by those who needed to pass through the woods by night, for the gloom and loneliness of such scenes led to superstitious fears. That is why a sudden fright without visible cause was blamed on Pan and was called a panic.

Yet Pan is said to have given the world a gift of great beauty and joy. Legend says that Pan invented music. It all began when he chased a nymph named Syrinx, who ran away from him across the fields and down to the riverbank. Syrinx was desired by many of the spirits and creatures of the woods, but she would have none of them.

Pan kept giving Syrinx compliments as he chased her. When she got to the bank of the river, she called for help from her friends, the

43

water nymphs. Just as Pan threw his arms around what he thought was Syrinx, he found he embraced only a tuft of reeds. As he breathed a sigh, the air sounded through the reeds and produced a plaintive melody. Charmed by the sweetness of the music, Pan gathered some reeds and placed them together in unequal lengths and made an instrument he named the Syrinx, in honor of the nymph.

Pan became fascinated by the music he played on his pipes. Full of his musical talents, he challenged the god of the lyre, Apollo, to a trial of musical skill. The judge of the contest was Apollo's friend, Tmolus, the mountain god. Pan blew upon his pipes and played a very pleasant rustic melody that captured the listeners. Apollo the sun god struck the strings of his lyre with his right hand and played a triumphant song of the sun and mountains. When he was done, Tmolus awarded the victory to Apollo.

Today when you listen to music played on the panpipes, listen for the sounds of the wind and imagine Pan as he danced on his cloven feet and played his reed instrument.

The flute is thought to have a special attraction for certain animals and aspects of nature and is the traditional instrument of shepherds.

A Shepherd Wins His Bride

(Turkey)

THERE ONCE WAS A POOR KURDISH shepherd who tended the flocks of a very wealthy man. He played lilting tunes on his flute while he watched the sheep. He would stroll among the crowds of sheep, playing his flute all the time. The sheep would stop munching grass when he was near just to listen to his music.

For the most part, this handsome young shepherd enjoyed his life. There was only one great sadness for him. The sheep sometimes heard sounds of this sadness in his songs. The cause of his sadness was the beautiful young daughter of the rich sheep owner. How he loved this fair maiden.

Sometimes she would travel up to where he was with the flocks to bring him some special cheese treat. Gaily colored ribbons fixed in her hair danced as she moved.

The maiden seemed to enjoy the shepherd's company as much as he enjoyed hers. During these visits they would sit together on the hillside and he would play his most entrancing music for her. Things progressed between them to the point where he talked to her of marriage.

"You know my father would never approve," she told him. "He plans for me to marry a rich old man in the village."

Full of fear but also love, the young shepherd went to the home of the sheep owner to ask to marry his daughter. "Kind sir, I love your beautiful daughter and am asking for your permission to marry her. She loves me, too, and we beg your blessings on becoming man and wife."

The girl's father grew angry and blustered around and scoffed at such an idea. The longer they talked, the more the father knew that this young shepherd was determined and would not be put off easily.

45

"All right! I have been impressed with your honesty and character. Therefore, I will consent to your wedding. There is only one condition. You must be able to keep my flock of 500 sheep from drinking for three days." The man knew how thirsty the sheep got and felt that this impossible condition would quiet all thoughts of marriage.

To his amazement, the shepherd said, "I agree to your condition. To win the hand of your daughter, nothing is impossible."

The shepherd sat on the hillside and began to play on his flute. He played the most enchanting and hypnotizing tunes he could create. Whenever a sheep would head toward the spring to take a drink, the flute player invented another soothing song that stopped the sheep in its tracks. The sheep recognized the music as their call and followed him away from the water. This went on for the full three days.

The father was amazed to see the power of the shepherd's music over the sheep. He watched for the three days and found that he himself sometimes fell under the spell of the songs. At the end of the third day the father joined the young man on the hillside and told him, "You have won my daughter as your wife. Anyone who can do what you have done is certainly a determined and talented man."

From that day onward, the young man and his descendants were known as the masters of the flute.

This is a story of magic, transformation, and hunting from the Yoruba tribe of Nigeria, Benin, and Togo in West Africa.

The Yoruba Flute
(Nigeria)

THE YORUBA HUNTER, Ojo, followed the tradition of long hunts in the forests of Nigeria, Benin, and Togo. Ojo would go deep into a forest to hunt. There he would build a camp using material gathered from the trees around him. His stick and palm frond camp served as a place for him to sleep as well as a place for him to cut up the animals he killed during the daily hunt. He would dry the meat of his catches over a fire of wood and glowing coals. Ojo would store the dry meat at his camp until he had enough to consider a successful hunt. In this way, with his bows and arrows as his weapons, he added to his food store.

Ojo was one of the best hunters in his village. His wife was pleased when he returned home after a successful hunt with his load of dried meat. She took the dried meat to the village market and traded it for things she and Ojo needed.

Beside his carefully crafted bows and arrows, Ojo had other hunting helpers. They were his three dogs and a very old flute. The dogs—Cut to Pieces, Swallow Up, and Clear the Remains—always ran to wherever Ojo was when they heard him blow on his magical flute.

Ojo almost always took his dogs with him on his long hunting trips, but one time he tied the dogs up at home and left them there. "Wife, please take care of my dogs while I am gone. If you should notice them acting unusually, let them free to follow me to where I am in the wilds of the forest."

"Yes, Ojo, if I notice the dogs becoming nervous or upset, I will do as you say," answered his wife.

Ojo traveled to a distant forest he had never hunted in before. Looking around him and studying the place, he decided that no other hunters had been to this place before. There were signs that this should be a bountiful hunt. With his trained eyes, Ojo discovered traces of many animals. As usual, he built his camp and made preparations for the hunt.

He felt uncomfortable, though, as he worked. It felt as though something was watching him. Whatever it was, he thought, was not people or animals. He decided that it was some powerful evil spirit spying on him. Ojo remembered the stories he had heard as a boy about forest spirits. Village men would sit around the evening cook fires and talk about the spirits they had seen. One villager with a deep, rich voice would whisper about the time he had seen Iyabomba, the mother of the forest. He said Iyabomba was as big as ten men and had hungry moving mouths all over her body.

Ojo began to grow fearful as he lay down that night. He still remembered the hushed voice of the villager as he described Iyabomba. And then it happened! The huge form of Iyabomba materialized before him. She looked just as evil as the storyteller's descriptions of her had been. Ojo froze in terror. Then he heard the main mouth of Iyabomba say, "I know why you have come to my forest. You plan to hunt here. Just know that if you do me no harm, I will not eat you. All will be well." And then she disappeared just as suddenly as she had arrived. All Ojo heard was a breeze moving the leaves of the trees.

The next morning Ojo started his hunt. He was relieved to be away from where he had seen Iyabomba. He had a very good hunt that day even though the fear was still with him.

Ojo returned to his camp with his kill and skinned and cut it all up. He gathered firewood and started a fire to dry the meat. He cooked some of the meat for his evening meal and then settled down for the night. The next day was the same, except that this time when he carried the day's kill into his camp, he noticed huge footprints that had to be those of Iyabomba. They led into his shelter and then he discovered that Iyabomba had taken all of the food he had stored there.

"Oh well," he thought. "Maybe that will satisfy Iyabomba. I have plenty of meat from today's hunt. Things should be fine." With that, he gathered wood, started a fire, and prepared the meat from the hunt.

After six days of hunting and returning to camp to find all his stored food gone, Ojo decided that even though this was the best hunting area he had ever seen, Iyabomba would probably continue to take his meat. "There is no sense in this," he mused to himself. "Tomorrow I will move my camp."

And so, Ojo did that. He started all over again in another part of the forest, but Iyabomba followed him there and took his food stores daily. Now instead of fear, Ojo felt deep anger. The next day he remained in his camp to wait for Iyabomba, but she never came. Ojo decided to break camp and leave. As he was organizing all of his goods, he mumbled, "You old hag! You have eaten all that I have worked for. Do you do that to every hardworking hunter who comes here?" With a loud crash, Iyabomba came toward him roaring with all of her mouths.

Ojo fled as fast as he could because he didn't want to become Iyabomba's next meal. "Come back so I can eat you," roared all of the mouths of Iyabomba. This just helped Ojo run faster, but it was no use. He knew that Iyabomba would soon snatch him up, so Ojo climbed up into the topmost branches of a great tree. He skinned his legs and arms as he scurried up the trunk.

Iyabomba looked up at him in the tree. She was not a tree climber, but she was a tree eater. All of her mouths started to tear at the bottom of the tree. As the tree swayed and pieces flew in every direction, Ojo remembered his magic flute. He blew a tune on it that he knew his dogs would hear.

Sure enough, back home Cut to Pieces, Swallow Up, and Clear the Remains heard the music. The three dogs started to howl. They became so agitated that they snapped their ropes before Ojo's wife could let them loose. She had heard their howls and remembered what Ojo had asked, but all she could do now was to watch the dogs leap over the mud walls of the compound and race off into the forest.

In great fear Ojo watched Iyabomba eating her way through the great tree. Branches fell, bark was shredded, and the tree was getting smaller. Ojo remembered something else that he had with him. It was a small leather bag that held some magic powder. He opened the bag and sprinkled some of the powder on the tree, and before his fearful eyes, the tree grew to its original size.

This startled Iyabomba but not for long. She just moved another part of her gigantic body toward the tree, and once more, many mouths attacked the tree. Every time the tree was almost destroyed, Ojo would sprinkle more of the magic powder on it and it would return to its former size. Iyabomba and Ojo did this time after time until all of the magic powder was gone and the tree was almost cut through once more.

Cut to Pieces, Swallow Up, and Clear the Remains appeared just as Ojo feared that the mother of the forest had won the battle. The three dogs threw themselves on Iyabomba with snarls and growls. Saliva flew everywhere as the fight raged, but at last Cut to Pieces, Swallow Up, and Clear the Remains killed Iyabomba. Of course, with names like theirs, the dogs knew what to do, and soon there were no traces left of Iyabomba.

Ojo climbed down the almost demolished tree, gathered up his belongings, and called to his three wonderful dogs. He could hardly wait to get home and tell his wife about the happenings when, suddenly, standing before him was a very beautiful woman. "Iyabomba held me as a prisoner and now, dear Ojo, that you have killed her and rescued me, I will become your wife," she said with a dazzling smile.

What happiness Ojo felt as he went back home with his hunting things, his dogs, and this lovely woman. Ojo's wife was happy to have them all home, and people in the village prepared a great feast and many celebrations when they heard that Iyabomba was dead. They were also pleased that Ojo's second wife had been set free from Iyabomba.

Back at home, Ojo and his two wives settled down to sleep. Then a terrible, strange thing happened. The beautiful woman quietly got up and started to change herself into an enormous creature with many moving mouths. It was the sister of Iyabomba. She had taken the shape of the lovely woman to avenge her sister's death. She was going to kill Ojo, his wife, and their three dogs. Then she would return to the forest and rule as her sister would have had she not been killed.

Before she could kill Ojo and his wife, Cut to Pieces, Swallow Up, and Clear the Remains sensed what was about to happen and started to bark an alarm. Ojo woke up just in time to see the dogs leap on the monster and tear her to pieces just as they had Iyabomba.

Ojo often went back to the part of the forest where he met Iyabomba, but he was never again troubled by forest spirits. He always returned from his hunts laden with meat. And so Ojo, his wife, and his dogs lived a happy life. Ojo treasured his magic flute and sometimes played music just for fun with it. When he did, his dogs always seemed to enjoy the music with him.

50

The Young Chief Who Played the Flute

(New Zealand)

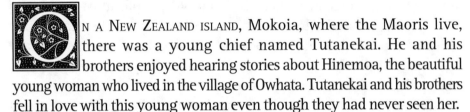

ON A NEW ZEALAND ISLAND, Mokoia, where the Maoris live, there was a young chief named Tutanekai. He and his brothers enjoyed hearing stories about Hinemoa, the beautiful young woman who lived in the village of Owhata. Tutanekai and his brothers fell in love with this young woman even though they had never seen her.

"I'm going to marry her someday," said one of the brothers.

"She is so gentle and beautiful, I must have her for my wife," said another brother.

Only Tutanekai said nothing, but in the evenings he would go to the top of the hillside and look across the water toward Owhata. He would take out his flute and play songs of tender love.

Sometimes Hinemoa heard these songs as she sat in the moonlight. She too had heard stories, but these were stories about the brothers of Mokoia. "That is Tutanekai playing the flute," she would say when she heard the love songs as they floated across the water.

It was festival time and the people of Mokoia paid a visit to Owhata. Tutanekai was among them, and it was then that he first saw the highborn Hinemoa. The stories about her had not done her justice.

And she recognized the tall, handsome young chief as the flute player of Mokoia. Their eyes met and the message was clear that they would meet that night, and they did in the shadow of the meeting house.

"Now that we have met, I cannot live without you," Tutanekai said. "When will we meet again?"

Hinemoa replied softly, "I will come to you, Tutanekai. My people will not allow me to marry you, but some night I will come to you when I have a chance. How shall I know when you will be waiting for me?"

51

Tutanekai thought for a moment. "You have heard my music with the message of my love across the waters. Now it can carry another message—the message that I am waiting for you. When you hear my flute music, you will know that I am waiting."

The next morning, the Mokoia visitors returned home. That night, when it was dark and all the people were asleep, Hinemoa crept down to the beach and looked around for a small canoe. She knew she could paddle such a canoe across to the island. But all of the canoes had been pulled out of the water and were dragged high up the beach. They were too heavy for her to move. This was very unusual, and she said to herself, "The old people must have seen how Tutanekai and I looked at each other. They must have done this to keep me from going to him." As she stood there, she heard the music of the flute. She listened to it and when it finally stopped, she sadly went back to her house.

Night after night Hinemoa went down to the beach as the sad love songs Tutanekai played on his flute drifted to her on the clear night air. Each night was the same; however, the canoes were always dragged high up on the beach.

How long would Tutanekai wait for her before he decided that she had forgotten him? At last Hinemoa could wait no longer. She would swim! She knew it was a long way to Mokoia, but she decided to swim to the island that night, in the dark. She collected some empty gourds, tied them under her arms, and waded out into the water.

The music from Tutanekai's flute came out of the dark night to guide her. Hinemoa swam steadily, but the waves splashed against her face and she couldn't hear the music. The water was cold. She became frightened now that she didn't know where she was.

She decided there was only one thing to do—keep on swimming. Once more she heard the flute calling to her and then the music stopped. Now there was only the sound of the waves splashing. There was no other sound in the night.

The water seemed to get colder, and then Hinemoa heard a new sound. It was the sound of waves lapping on a stony beach. This gave her hope and she quickly swam to the beach and felt her way in front of her with her hands. She brushed through low bushes and felt the rocks. The rocks were warm and then she smelled the steam from a hot pool. Now she knew where she was.

The hot pool was near Tutanekai's home. She stepped into the pool and lay down so the water warmed her cold body. As she lay there she started to feel quite shy. Her clothes were far away on the beach at Owhata and she did not dare to go to Tutanekai's house without clothes. Just as she was thinking all of this and trying to figure out what to do, she heard someone coming. She quickly hid behind a big rock. In the dark she could not see anything, but she heard footsteps and a splash as a calabash was lowered into the pool.

"Where are you taking the water?" she said in a deep voice like a man. "Who are you?"

The startled man answered, "I am taking the water to Tutanekai."

In the same deep voice Hinemoa said, "Give me the calabash." She waded up to him and took the calabash which she threw so that it crashed on the rocks and broke into many pieces.

Tutanekai's serving man cried out angrily, "Why have you done that? That was Tutanekai's calabash!"

Hinemoa had hidden behind the rock again and didn't answer. The man began to think that it must have been an evil spirit that had broken the calabash, so he ran back to Tutanekai's house and told him what had happened.

"Who broke the calabash?" asked Tutanekai.

"The man at the pool," replied the man.

"Yes, but who was this man?"

"I don't know. I couldn't see his face but he had the voice of a man," said Tutanekai's serving man.

For a brief time Tutanekai thought of going down to see for himself but then he thought, what did it matter? He had other thoughts on his mind. Night after night he had played to Hinemoa, and night after night he had strained to see her canoe, but she had not come. Maybe she had forgotten him!

"It doesn't matter," Tutanekai said to his serving man. "Take another calabash, but make sure that you bring it back this time."

Carefully, the serving man went back to the hot pool but as soon as he reached the water the deep voice demanded, "If that is Tutanekai's calabash, give it to me!"

He replied, "No, I promised to take this back to Tutanekai."

"Give it to me," Hinemoa said fiercely, and the serving man, who still feared that this person with the deep voice might be an evil spirit, handed it over. Again, Hinemoa smashed the calabash on the rocks. This time the poor man ran up the path and stumbled into Tutanekai's house.

"Master, the second calabash has gone too," he said. "It was the same man in the hot pool who took it and smashed it."

"Never mind," Tutanekai said wearily. "We have plenty of calabashes. Take another and see how it goes this time."

The frightened man was soon back empty-handed again. This time Tutanekai was really angry. "I will put a stop to this!" he said. He threw off his sleeping mat, grabbed his club, and ran down to the pool.

Hinemoa heard him coming and knew that this time it was her beloved, because the serving man's footsteps had been heavy and slow, while Tutanekai ran lightly and swiftly. She hid behind the rock and held her breath as her lover reached the edge of the pool. The moon was rising, and she saw his shadow across the water. "Where are you, breaker of pots?" called Tutanekai. "Come out so that I can see you. Show yourself like a man instead of hiding like a crayfish in the water."

Hinemoa did not answer. She could see Tutanekai's shadow moving across the water, coming closer and closer. A hand reached down and touched her hair. "Ah ha!" said Tutanekai, thinking that he had found the rascal who had broken his calabashes. "Come out into the light and fight like a man!"

Tutanekai pulled harder and said angrily, "Let me see your face."

Then Hinemoa stood up shyly like a white heron that is seen only once in a hundred years. She stood in the pool amid the bright moonlight.

The club fell from Tutanekai's hand and dangled at his side by its flax string. He stepped back in amazement and then held out his arms. Hand in hand the two went up the path to Tutanekai's home and were married that very night.

The next morning as the sun rose and steam from the ovens rose straight up in the still air, someone noticed that Tutanekai was not there. "Where is he?" they asked, but no one had seen him.

"There is his serving man, let's ask him," said an old woman.

"I do not know," said the serving man. "The door of his home is closed, and I have not seen him since he went down to see the stranger at the hot pool last night."

The people asked him about the stranger and he told them about the smashed calabashes. "The last I saw of angry Tutanekai, he told me to stay here and then he took his club and went down to the hot pool."

Everyone looked at each other. One old man stood and said, "These are strange words. Perhaps something has happened to him. He is a brave fighter, but the night was dark, and the stranger may well have lain in wait for Tutanekai and maybe killed him. I say that some of the young men should go down to the pool to see if he is there."

One young man said, "Those are wise words, my father, but perhaps Tutanekai is still in his home. See, the door is still shut. I think we should look in there first."

"Yes, yes, yes," said the people. "Let us look there first."

The serving man went to the house and slid the door back and looked inside for a very long time. He returned to the others. "There are four feet there. I looked for Tutanekai and I saw four feet instead of two."

"Well then, who is with him?" the old woman asked.

The serving man went back and looked through the door again. He went right inside, and then he came out. As he walked back to the people, they could see that he was excited.

"I have seen her! It is Hinemoa!" he announced.

The old woman asked, "Hinemoa who lives at Owhata?"

"Yes, it is her. Tutanekai has been courting her. She must have heard the music of his flute and come to him from across the lake."

They all shouted "Welcome!" to Hinemoa, and that night Hinemoa told them how she had crossed the lake by swimming through the dark water, guided by the music of Tutanekai's flute. From that day on, Hinemoa and Tutanekai enjoyed the music of the flute together. When they had children, their children danced on the sandy beach as Tutanekai played gentle love songs for them.

Wolfgang Amadeus Mozart composed the music for the opera The Magic Flute *(or* Die Zauberflote*) during the last year of his life. The libretto, written by Emanuel Schikaneder, was based on "Lulu" or "The Magic Flute," a fairy tale by German poet Cristoph Wieland.*

The Magic Flute

(Germany)

IT WAS A WARM SPRING DAY, and Prince Lulu was riding his favorite horse in a meadow full of flowers. Prince Lulu was amazed at the sight of a white gazelle that appeared like magic in front of him. He had never seen such a beautiful creature in all of his young life. "I must follow this magical gazelle and find out where it lives," he thought.

The gazelle led him through forests, across streams, and over mountains. When they went through a forest that had no sunlight reaching the ground because of the huge, abundant trees, the gazelle seemed to slow down so Prince Lulu could keep up with it. When they crossed streams, the gazelle seemed to pick out the easiest spots for the crossing to help Prince Lulu. "I think this magical creature wants me to follow it," he decided.

They traveled like this for a long distance until the prince found himself in a strange land. They drew near a castle on the point of a steep mountain that was different from any other castle. It gleamed and seemed to sparkle with dancing lights.

When they got to the castle, the gazelle led Prince Lulu through the imposing gates, and then the creature seemed to disappear as magically as it had appeared. Prince Lulu was taken into the presence of the castle's owner, the fairy Perifirime. Prince Lulu had never seen a fairy before, but Perifirime was probably unusual even among fairies. They talked for a long while over a table full of enticing food and drink. Prince Lulu didn't know how hungry he was until fairy attendants brought the trays and trays of meat, fruit, and other delicious things he had never eaten before.

"I see that you are just the person I need to help me," Perifirime stated. "You are not only modest, courageous, and wise, but also innocent. I have a quest that requires these very virtues. An evil magician named Dilsenghuin has stolen my magic tinderbox. Its magical powers must not be discovered by such an evil one as he. If you recover the tinderbox from Dilsenghuin, I will give you the best of my possessions."

Prince Lulu was pleased to be entrusted with such a special task. Perifirime left the room and returned with some objects that she presented to Prince Lulu. "Here is a magic flute. It has the power to win the love of all who hear it and to incite or still all passions that its player wishes. It is worth more than gold and crowns. In a magic hour, my father carved it from the deepest core of the thousand-year-old oak in lightning and thunder, storm and din. He put six keys on it of solid gold."

Then she handed Prince Lulu a ring. "This is not just an ordinary ring. If turned on your finger it will make you appear young or old. If it is thrown from you, it will summon help immediately."

"Now let us begin the search for my magic tinderbox." Saying this, Perifirime led Prince Lulu to a chariot of clouds. In it they traveled most of the way to the dark castle of the magician, Dilsenghuin. "You must be careful of Dilsenghuin. Not only is he evil, but he also has an extremely suspicious nature. Worst of all, he is holding a girl prisoner and is trying to win her love," warned the fairy. "Be careful and use your wisdom to achieve your goal."

As the cloud-chariot floated away, Prince Lulu decided that it might be wise to disguise himself. Because he had the magic flute, he chose the role of a minstrel. When he turned the ring on his finger he said "Minstrel," and that is just what he appeared to be.

He tried the flute out as he traveled to the castle. At one point he came upon two men, who were leading their cows to market while engaged in a loud fight. He played a tune that had the immediate effect of gentling them into a more friendly mood. The next person Prince Lulu saw on the road was an unhappy man. The tune he played brightened the mood for the man until he was actually dancing a lively dance to the music.

At the great iron gate to the castle, Prince Lulu announced to the gatekeeper that he had heard about the magician's efforts to win the love of the girl he had captured. "I have come to use my flute to gain the girl's love for Dilsenghuin. She will not be able to resist my music," the prince promised. The ambitious gatekeeper led the minstrel to Dilsenghuin, hoping that the musician was right and would do what he claimed.

Prince Lulu repeated his promise to Dilsenghuin. "But first, I need to talk with this precious lady," he said. He was led into her chambers and at once recognized why the magician sought her love. Sidi was the most beautiful maiden Prince Lulu had ever seen.

"Dear Sidi," he confided to her, "I am here to recover the fairy Perifirime's magic tinderbox, but I think I also must rescue you from the evil one." Lulu told Sidi his plan to beat Dilsenghuin and instructed her on the ring's power.

"Are you ready to marry me?" roared the magician as soon as Prince Lulu and Sidi returned to face him. "Has the minstrel created love in you for me?"

Sidi asked the magician, "May I see the wonderful magic tinderbox? Maybe the sight of the box will help me make up my mind."

Dilsenghuin didn't trust any of his servants to get the box, so he himself eagerly went to his treasure room. He unlocked the door, which had nine heavy locks on it. He took the tinderbox from its place on a crystal stand and returned to Sidi. "For your love, dear Sidi, I would do anything."

Sidi, instead of being gentle and agreeable, firmly told the magician, "I would never, ever agree to marry such an evil one as you. In fact, I will return this box to its rightful owner." Saying this, she seized the tinderbox and threw the ring Lulu had given her out a window.

Perifirime appeared and punished the astonished Dilsenghuin and his cohorts. The fairy then took Lulu and Sidi back to her castle. It was a time for many miracles. Prince Lulu was surprised to find his father and Sidi's father waiting for a great celebration. "What is the celebration that brings you all here?" asked Prince Lulu.

"The marriage of our children is worthy of such a gathering," Lulu's father told him. With that Prince Lulu took out his magic flute and played music of love that cast a spell over all who heard it. It was the most loving wedding that was ever held on earth or in fairyland.

Suggestions for Extending Experiences

♪ Collect a file of pictures of all kinds of flutes and panpipes from around the world. Review the file when appropriate and make a chart listing the name, country, type of instrument, size, material, number of holes, and other characteristics of each instrument.

♪ Experiment with various materials for flute making, such as straws, reeds, pipes, bamboo, macaroni, and so forth. How does the placement of holes affect the musical scale?

♪ Experiment with vibration, sound, and pitch using a variety of materials.

♪ Share Claude Clement's *Musician from the Darkness* (Boston: Little, Brown, 1988). Then read stories about flute making and write your own original story telling how flutes came to be. Tell your story to family or friends.

♪ Read aloud Phillis Gershator's *Tukama Tootles the Flute: A Tale from the Antilles* (New York: Orchard Books, 1994). Make johnnycake by mixing together 1 egg, 2 cups cornmeal, 3/4 teaspoon salt, and 1 1/2 cups milk. Drop spoonfuls of batter onto a greased, hot griddle. Fry until brown on both sides. Serve with butter, powdered sugar, or both.

♪ Rewrite "The Gift of the Elk" as a readers theatre production.

♪ Find and listen to recordings that feature the flute. For example, the flute and pennywhistle music of James Galway would be an excellent resource.

♪ Purchase a pennywhistle at a music store. Learn to play a variety of easy tunes. How does the pennywhistle compare to the instruments you have made?

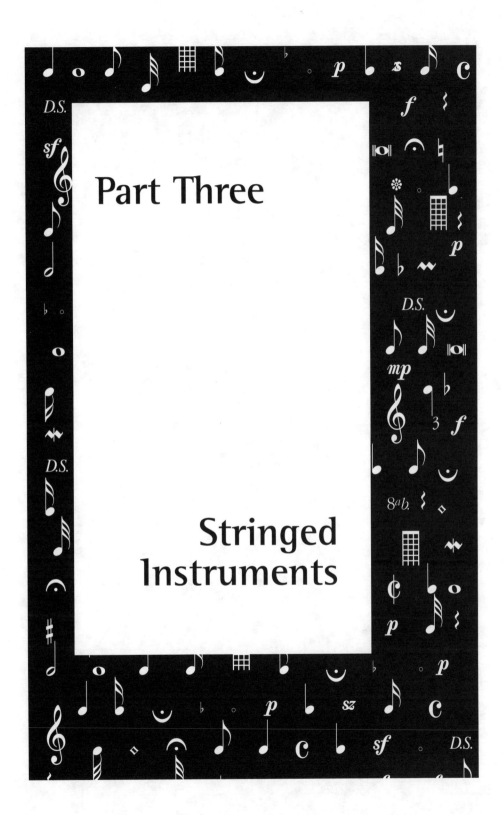

Part Three

Stringed Instruments

A strong woman who plays the lute uses her music to save her husband, the king.

The Lute Player

(Russia)*

NCE UPON A TIME there were a king and a queen who lived happily and comfortably together. They were very fond of each other and had nothing to worry them, but at last the king grew restless. He longed to go out into the world, to try his strength in battle against some enemy, and to win all kinds of honor and glory.

So he called his army together and gave orders to start for a distant country where a heathen king ruled who mistreated or tormented everyone he could lay his hands on. The king then gave his parting orders and wise advice to his ministers, took a tender leave of his wife, and set off with his army across the sea.

I cannot say whether the voyage was short or long; but at last he reached the country of the heathen king and marched on, defeating all who came in his way. But this did not last long, for in time he came to a mountain pass, where a large army was waiting for him, who put his soldiers to flight, and took the king himself prisoner.

He was carried off to the prison where the heathen king kept his captives, and now our poor friend had a very bad time indeed. All night long the prisoners were chained up, and in the morning they were yoked together like oxen and had to plough the land till it grew dark.

This state of things went on for three years before the king found any means of sending news of himself to his dear queen, but at last he contrived to send this letter: "Sell all our castles and palaces, and put all our treasures in pawn and come and deliver me out of this horrible prison."

The queen received the letter, read it, and wept bitterly as she said to herself, "How can I deliver my dearest husband? If I go myself and the heathen king sees me he will just take me to be one

63

of his wives. If I were to send one of the ministers!—but I hardly know if I can depend on them."

She thought, and thought, and at last an idea came into her head. She cut off all her beautiful long brown hair and dressed herself in boy's clothes. Then she took her lute and, without saying anything to anyone, she went forth into the wide world.

She traveled through many lands and saw many cities, and went through many hardships before she got to the town where the heathen king lived. When she got there she walked all round the palace and at the back she saw the prison. Then she went into the great court in front of the palace, and taking her lute in her hand, she began to play so beautifully that one felt as though one could never hear enough.

After she had played for some time she began to sing, and her voice was sweeter than the lark's.

> I come from my own country far
> Into this foreign land,
> Of all I own I take alone
> My sweet lute in my hand.
>
> Oh! who will thank me for my song,
> Reward my simple lay?
> Like lovers' sighs it still shall rise
> To greet thee day by day.
>
> I sing of blooming flowers
> Made sweet by sun and rain;
> Of all the bliss of love's first kiss,
> And parting's cruel pain.
>
> Of the sad captive's longing
> Within his prison wall,
> Of hearts that sigh when none are nigh
> To answer to their call.
>
> My songs beg for your pity,
> And gifts from out your store,
> And as I play my gentle lay
> I linger near your door.

And if you hear my singing
Within your palace, sire,
Oh! give, I pray, this happy day,
To me my heart's desire.

No sooner had the heathen king heard this touching song sung by such a lovely voice, than he had the singer brought before him.

"Welcome, O lute player," said he. "Where do you come from?"

"My country, sire, is far away across many seas. For years I have been wandering about the world and gaining my living by my music."

"Stay here then a few days, and when you wish to leave I will give you what you ask for in your song—your heart's desire."

So the lute player stayed on in the palace and sang and played almost all day long to the king, who could never tire of listening and almost forgot to eat or drink or to torment people. He cared for nothing but the music, and nodded his head as he declared, "That's something like playing and singing. It makes me feel as if some gentle hand had lifted every care and sorrow from me."

After three days the lute player came to take leave of the king.

"Well," said the king, "what do you desire as your reward?"

"Sire, give me one of your prisoners. You have so many in your prison, and I should be glad of a companion on my journeys. When I hear his happy voice as I travel along I shall think of you and thank you."

"Come along then," said the king, "choose whom you will." And he took the lute player through the prison himself.

The queen walked about among the prisoners, and at length she picked out her husband and took him with her on her journey. They were long on their way, but he never found out who she was, and she led him nearer and nearer to his own country.

When they reached the frontier, the prisoner said, "Let me go now, kind lad. I am no common prisoner, but the king of this country. Let me go free and ask what you will as your reward."

"Do not speak of reward," answered the lute player. "Go in peace."

"Then come with me, dear boy, and be my guest."

"When the proper time comes I shall be at your palace," was the reply, and so they parted.

The queen took a short way home, got there before the king, and changed her dress.

An hour later all the people in the palace were running to and fro and crying out, "Our king has come back! Our king has returned to us."

The king greeted everyone very kindly, but he could not so much as look at the queen.

Then he called all his council and ministers together and said to them, "See what sort of a wife I have. Here she is falling on my neck, but when I was pining in prison and sent her word of it, she did nothing to help me."

And his council answered with one voice, "Sire, when news was brought from you, the queen disappeared and no one knew where she went. She only returned today."

Then the king was very angry and cried, "Judge my faithless wife! Never would you have seen your king again if a young lute player had not delivered him. I shall remember him with love and gratitude as long as I live."

While the king was sitting with his council, the queen found time to disguise herself. She took her lute, and slipping into the court in front of the palace she sang, clear and sweet:

> I sing the captive's longing
> Within his prison wall,
> Of hearts that sigh when none are nigh
> To answer to their call.
>
> My song begs for your pity,
> And gifts from out your store,
> And as I play my gentle lay
> I linger near your door.
>
> And if you hear my singing
> Within your palace, sire,
> Oh! give, I pray, this happy day,
> To me my heart's desire.

As soon as the king heard this song, he ran out to meet the lute player, took him by the hand and led him into the palace.

"Here," he cried, "is the boy who released me from my prison. And now, my true friend, I will indeed give you your heart's desire."

"I am sure you will not be less generous than the heathen king was, sire. I ask of you what I asked and obtained from him. But this time I don't mean to give up what I get. I want you—yourself!"

And as she spoke she threw off her long cloak and everyone saw it was the queen.

Who can tell how happy the king was? In the joy of his heart he gave a great feast to the whole world, and the whole world came and rejoiced with him for a whole week.

I was there too, and ate and drank many good things. I shan't forget that feast as long as I live.

From "The Lute Player," in Wise Women: Folk and Fairy Tales from Around the World *by Suzanne I. Barchers (Englewood, CO: Libraries Unlimited, 1990); and* Violet Fairy Book, *edited by Andrew Lang (New York: Dover Publications, 1966).*

According to their neighbors, Finns are wizards and witches who control wind, rain, and frost. People in the Middle Ages spoke of Finns carrying the wind around in a bag or bringing a storm under control by tying three knots in a rope. Here is a story of the oldest of the ancient wizards of Finland.

Vainamoinen, the Singer, and His Harp

(Finland)*

VAINAMOINEN, the oldest of the ancient wizards, was born of the virgin maiden Ilmatar of the air, a spirit of nature who had come down to the open space. The winds blew her pregnant. It took 700 years for this pregnancy to be born as the seas. Ilmatar fashioned the earth and all that is on it from the sea, so she became known as the Mother of the Sea. Again the winds blew her pregnant, and for thirty years, Vainamoinen grew in her womb. His wisdom helped him find his way out and he was born into the sea and waves. There he rolled among the billows for eight years. And so, the eternal sage and stouthearted singer began his adventures.

Ancient Finns believed in the magical existence of words, the utterance of which made anything accomplished. You built a house by uttering certain magical words. You made a horse out of bits of bark and old sticks by singing certain magical songs over them. Whole armies of men might be created in a moment by the utterance of these magical words. Words, songs, and magic explained the world. Vainamoinen was like all Finns. He knew the magic of words and music.

On one of his many adventures, Vainamoinen found himself in a boat in some swift rapids, and the boat got stuck on the back of a big pike. He sang:

> The boat is on a pike's shoulders,
> On the shoulder blades of a dog of the water,
> Let us sweep the water with a sword,
> Cut the fish in two.

68

He drew his sword and thrust it into the sea and dug into the pike's shoulders. He pulled the pike out of the water, but his sword had cut deeply. The pike broke in two pieces with the tail falling to the water, and the main part into the skiff.

Vainamoinen cut the fish into pieces. He decided to make a harp, an instrument of eternal joy, from the great pike's jawbone. He made pegs for the harp from the pike's teeth, and the harp strings were made from hairs of the devil's horse.

Everyone came to look at the fishbone harp. They tried to play it, but the music did not rise to the point of joyous music. The strings kinked up and the horsehairs squeaked badly. It sounded terrible.

Then the harp strings sang out:

> You make me shudder,
> Bring me to the hands of he who made me,
> I seek the fingers of the tuner.

The people carried the harp to Vainamoinen. Vainamoinen, the steadfast, eternal singer took the instrument in his fingers and began to delicately play the pikebone harp. Rapture after rapture burst forth. The pike's teeth rang out, the hairs resounded, and joyous music sang out clearly. As Vainamoinen played, there was not a creature of nature or the forest that did not come to hear and marvel at the music. There were squirrels, weasels, elk, lynx, wolf, and bear cavorting to the music. The spirits of the woodland all came to listen to the harp. Birds soared on two wings, whirling, hurrying, and marveling. Even the eagle began to fly to the playing. It flew on high along with the swans, chaffinches, buntings, and larks.

There was not a creature of the water, land, or air that did not come to listen. Voices in the wind said, "Never before have I heard anything of this sort." As Vainamoinen played, there was not a person who did not start to weep. Hearts melted. The sound was delightful and wonderful. Even Vainamoinen had teardrops trickling from his eyes that were bigger than cranberries, rounder than grouse eggs. Teardrops flowed from beside Vainamoinen to the shore of the blue sea, to under the clear waters and onto the black ooze.

Vainamoinen offered a reward to any creature who could gather his tears from the sea. Finally, after many others tried, the blue goldeneye gathered them and brought them to Vainamoinen's hand, but they had been changed to other things. They swelled up into pearls, bluish freshwater pearls that would become an honor for kings as well as an everlasting joy.

On one of the great adventures in which Vainamoinen traveled to the North Farm to recover the Sampo or magic mill from the mistress of the North Farm, she created a dense fog and a huge gale. In the storm, Vainamoinen's harp disappeared into the sea. He mourned, "There has gone my creation, my lovely instrument, my eternal source of joy! I will never, never have such a clear-toned fishbone instrument."

After safely returning to Kalevala, Vainamoinen asked the craftsman Ilmarinen to forge an iron rake with close-set teeth and a long handle so he could rake the ocean to get his instrument back. Ilmarinen forged an iron rake with a copper handle, teeth 100 fathoms long, and a handle 500 fathoms long. Vainamoinen set off in a new boat. He sang:

> Set out, boat,
> For the water,
> Take yourself to the waves,
> No arm will turn you,
> No thumb will guide you.

Vainamoinen raked up water lilies, shore rubbish, bits of sedge, and litter of rushes, but he could not find his pikebone harp. The vanished harp was forever lost and would no longer make joyous music. As Vainamoinen sadly walked toward home, he said, "There is probably nothing left of the pike-tooth source of joyous music, the clear-toned fishbone instrument."

Then he heard a curly grained birch tree weeping and saw it shedding tears. He went to it and asked, "Why are you weeping, lovely birch? Why are you crying, green tree? Why are you lamenting, white-girdled one? No one is taking you to war. No one wants you for combat."

"I anguish because someone might peel my bark, pull my leafy branches off, slash me with knives, or use me for a berry basket!" spoke the tree. "Evil times and dark days are coming. Night chill and wind will take my leaves. I will be naked to shiver in the cold and to shriek in the frost."

"Do not weep, green tree! You will get abundant good fortune, get a pleasanter new life. Soon you will rejoice in your new happiness." With that old Vainamoinen fashioned the birch into a harp. He carved the body of the harp, the frame of the new source of joyous music, from the body of the tough birch. An oak was growing in the cattle yard, and he made harp pegs from the golden balls of acorns. He made screws for the frame from the curly birch, and then set out looking for something to use for strings.

He came upon a virgin sitting in the clearing, singing to while away her afternoon in the hope that her suitor was coming. Vainamoinen went to her to beg for hairs.

> Give me, virgin,
> Some of your hair,
> Some of your tresses,
> To be strings for a harp,
> To be the voice of immortal music.

She did and so her hairs became the strings of the immortal instrument. When it was finished Vainamoinen seated himself on a solid rock where he took the harp in his hands. He adjusted the strings and regulated the tones. When he played the harp, the curly birchwood sang out. It resounded, mountains echoed, boulders crashed, and all the crags shook. Rocks splashed into the ocean and gravel boiled in the water. Pine trees rejoiced and tree stumps jumped about on the heath. People marveled at the joyous music and stood with their cheeks on their hands. Tears flowed, and everyone with one voice said:

> Before now such lovely playing
> Has never been heard,
> Never, never at all
> While the moon has been gold-bright.

Wild animals came to listen. Forest animals squatted on their claws, birds settled down on twigs, fish came to the shore, and even grubs in the ground moved up to the surface of the soil.

Vainamoinen played one day. He played a second at one stretch with a single morning meal. He played at home in his cabin of evergreen logs. Trees frolicked, flowers became sportively joyful, and young saplings bent over.

Many years and adventures later, Vainamoinen prepared to depart forever. He bequeathed the harp and his great songs to the people of Finland. He got in his copper boat, and as he sailed away he sang:

> I meadowlark, got to wandering.
> I must rove about
> To feel every wind
> To shiver in the cold.
> To scream out in the severe frost.
> I blazed a trail for singers,
> Blazed a trail that broke off tree tops,
> Broke branches to show the way.
> A new course stretches out
> For more clever singers,
> For ampler songs,
> In the rising younger generation,
> Among the people growing up.

And so Vainamoinen left his people, traveling in a place between heaven and earth where he still is. No one knows where he is or when he will return. His music has not been heard lately, but parts of his songs are remembered and sung even now. If you are worthy, you may one day hear them again.

Adapted from the Finnish epic, The Kalevala, *collected by Elias Lonnrot.*

The harp was believed to have strong powers over its listeners and to dispel the spirits of evil. The festival harp is the national emblem of Ireland.

The Legend of the Irish Harp

(Ireland)

NE MISTY DAY, a young woman with black hair and the bluest of eyes was walking along the beach. She was idly collecting pretty pebbles and shells. The mists moved in and out from the water as she strolled, softly singing romantic songs to herself. She thought of her handsome husband as she sang.

She had just walked up to a patch of reeds when she heard music sweeter than anything she had ever heard in her life. She pushed past the reeds and there found the skeleton of a whale. The sweet music she was hearing was coming from the skeleton.

As she came along the side of the whale, she discovered that the music was caused by the wind singing ever so sweetly through the bones of the whale. The music was hypnotizing, and before the girl knew it she slumped to the ground and was lulled to sleep.

Her husband came home from his work in the fields expecting to find his young wife in their cozy kitchen brewing him a pot of tea. They enjoyed sharing a quiet cup of tea together at this time of day and telling each other the events of the day.

Time passed and his wife didn't appear, so the man went out to search for her. He started along the beach, because he knew she enjoyed walking there. She must have had such a pleasing walk that she had forgotten how late it was.

He saw her prints in the sand leading out toward the bay and followed them. He heard some unearthly music as he came near a patch of reeds. On the other side of the reeds, he found his dear wife peacefully sleeping beside the skeleton of a whale. He too saw that the enchanting music came from the wind on the whale bones.

The husband gently woke his wife up and together they reveled in the music. When the wind stopped blowing, the music stopped, but not before the husband had observed the principle behind the music.

Back at home, he secretly made a harp to imitate those sounds they had heard. When it was finished, he presented it to his wife with a flourish and a love song he sang and played for her. And that is how the first Irish harp came to be.

Where did the Gypsies get their most beloved instrument, the fiddle?

How the Fiddle Came to the Gypsies

(Gypsy)

IN A TIME WHEN the only music of the night was that of courting frogs, insects, and the wind in the leaves, Gypsies told this story around their crackling fires. The story is about both the good and the bad. You will know which is which when you hear it.

There was once a very beautiful girl who was also foolish, silly, and somewhat bewitched. Everyone was surprised that a girl of such beauty was not married until they got to know how foolish she was.

She was in love with the handsome young man who lived next door to her. He wanted nothing to do with such a silly girl, though. He never asked her to dance and tried to keep out of her way. Everyone recognized this, including the girl, and it made her sad.

One day when she was particularly sad and weepy over being ignored by the one she loved, the girl took a walk in the forest. Have you ever heard anyone singing a song while weeping at the same time? That was what she was doing as she went.

From nowhere, there appeared a man dressed all in green with burning black eyes and two little horns sticking out of the black hair on his head. His feet were like the cloven hoofs of a goat. Of course, this had to be the evil one, himself.

"I know why you are crying," he said. "If you will do one little thing for me, I will help you in return. This young man you love will not only love you in return, but he will ask you to marry him."

The girl stopped crying immediately. "If this could only come to be! I will do whatever you want. My dream is that he will love me as I love him."

"Ha! We have a bargain then. All I ask is that you give me your parents and four brothers. I will give you an amazing instrument and teach you how to play it. Whenever your beloved hears you play it, he will love you desperately and do anything in the world for you," promised the evil one.

"Of course you can have my parents and brothers! I will give you anything if only my love becomes mine. I have a kitten I love that you can have, also," the foolish girl replied.

In a poof and a puff, the evil one changed the girl's father into a fiddle. He then changed the mother into a bow and used her own snow white hair for the strings of the bow. Did you ever wonder why there were four strings on a fiddle? Well, that was because he changed her four brothers into the strings.

The girl admired the fiddle but of course couldn't make any music with it. The evil one was a master teacher, though, and soon she played music that made the birds stop flying to perch on the tree branches to listen. Her music made the frogs in the pond start dancing on the lily pads. It was the kind of music that brought misty, moist tears to the eyes. It was like no other music ever heard.

The strains of the music floated everywhere, and the young man of her dreams heard it. The haunting refrains made him forget everything. Even though he was a good worker, he forgot all about work and took to dancing. He sought the girl out and proposed to her immediately.

They lived very happily together for many years. Just as the music of the fiddle does to this day, it drove away all sadness and troubles. Life was full of joy for them. Then one summer day, the evil one came back. The couple had gone berry picking and had left the fiddle at home. When they returned home with buckets of juicy raspberries, they discovered the fiddle was gone. It was nowhere to be found. They turned the house apart looking for it, but the devil had taken it and hidden it.

They heard a carriage drive up in front of their home and ran out to see what it was. There were four shining black horses pulling a black carriage. The couple disappeared and was never seen again.

The fiddle lay hidden in the woods for many years until it was covered with moss and leaves. There is no way to know how many years it lay there. And then it happened. A band of Gypsies camped in the forest. As some of the boys were gathering tree branches and sticks for the fire, one of them accidentally hit the strings of the fiddle with a stick. The sound it made was the most beautiful sound the boy had ever heard, but he ran off in fright. The sound haunted him and so he gathered all his courage and went back. He found the fiddle and the bow hidden under the moss and leaves. He instinctively knew to move the bow across the strings. As he did this, the most magical inviting sounds issued forth. The boy began to think up tunes in his head that he started playing on the fiddle. He became the first Gypsy fiddler, making music that brought joy and happiness to all who heard it.

Back at the camp, the boy played his music for his band of Gypsies. He was able to cast spells over his listeners by making them sad with sad tunes and spirited and wild when he played wild music. Quickly other Gypsies learned to play the fiddle. Those who learned taught others, and today the Gypsies are recognized for their heavenly melodies and zesty tunes.

Only the fiddle can make such music, and so whenever you are among the Gypsies, you will always hear them making musical magic with their beloved instrument.

This violin story comes from the Hispanic Southwest.

The Magic Violin

(United States)*

NE DAY A LITTLE SHEPHERD BOY was in the field, tending to his sheep. He enjoyed being out in the field with the sheep because the world was always so peaceful there. The animals got along, and on some days the smell of the flowers made the little boy think he was in heaven itself. When the evening sunset came, with its beautiful painted sky, he knew that the Lord was in heaven, looking after his own flock on earth.

The little boy was an orphan child. His parents had been killed right after he was born, and he had been taken in by the wealthiest man in the valley. The man owned the largest ranch around; he was well known in the valley for his land and the size of his herds.

The man had taken in the little boy as an act of charity. At the time he had said, "I can always use another shepherd, as long as he doesn't eat too much." The man had always thought this was the funniest joke, but as the little boy grew older, he hated hearing it because it reminded him that he was an orphan child.

The little boy would go out with the sheep and would not come back to the ranch for days on end. He felt much better being with the sheep, where he didn't have to listen to his master make jokes about him. The little boy told himself that one day he would be able to go out on his own and stop living with his master. He knew that this would be the happiest day of his life.

One day while he was out with the sheep, he heard singing coming from the top of the hill. He had never heard such beautiful singing, and was surprised that anyone would be as far out in the field as he was. He had chosen that spot to feed the sheep because it was so far away from everything.

He climbed to the top of the hill, and there was a woman dressed in a shimmering white gown. Around her head was a circle of light, and she seemed to be floating off the ground.

The little boy asked the lady, "Who are you? And why are you here, so far from everything?"

The lady answered in a voice that seemed to be as light as the air, "I am the Blessed Virgin Mary, the mother of Jesus Christ. I have been watching over you since your parents died. Your parents are in heaven now, and they asked me to watch over you. I know how lonely you have been, and I have come to give you a present to entertain you during your long times alone."

She gave him a violin. It was a small violin, just his size, made of light brown wood. The little boy told the Virgin, "But I don't know how to play the violin."

The Virgin comforted him with her words. "You will learn how. Besides, this is not an ordinary violin. It is a special violin. Whenever you play it, everyone will dance. They will keep dancing until you stop playing. Enjoy your gift and know that I am watching after you."

The little boy started to say something to the Virgin, but she just disappeared while he stood there watching her. He could not believe that he had been so lucky. This violin would be his special friend, and he would play it to make the sheep happy.

During his long days and nights with the sheep, he played the violin, and a peacefulness came over the land whenever he played.

When he finally returned to the ranch, he found all of his things packed up and thrown outside the bunkhouse. He asked who had done this, and the ranch boss told him, "The master said you are getting too old and eating too much. He's fired you, and you are to go on your own way."

The little boy didn't care that he had been fired. He was old enough to go out on his own, and anyway, this was the day he had been waiting for. He went to the master and asked for the wages that the master owed him.

The master told him, "Wages! I don't owe you anything. I took you in when you were an orphan baby, and all these years I have fed you and given you a place to sleep."

The boy protested, "But you promised me wages when I started taking care of the sheep. You owe me my wages!"

The master cuffed the boy on the head and said, "Get out before I call the sheriff and tell him you've been stealing."

The boy knew that it was wrong for the master to refuse to pay him, but he was so frightened he ran away as fast as he could. He took his belongings and his little violin and left the ranch forever.

He went into town and asked if there was any work. The owner of an inn said that he needed a boy to wash dishes, and that he could have the job if he wanted it. The boy was really happy that he had found a job so easily, and then he remembered that the Virgin was watching over him. He went to church every day to thank the Virgin and to pray for the souls of his parents.

One evening the master came to the inn to eat. As usual he brought a lot of friends with him, and they had a large dinner party. The master did not know that the boy was working in the back of the kitchen of the inn.

During a break from his work, the boy took out his violin and played a soft and gentle song. The people in the inn heard the tune and were so moved by its beauty that they began to dance. The dancing wound around the tables, and everyone began to sing along with the song, until the inn became very noisy with the sound of singing and dancing.

The boy heard all the noise, and when he peeked out the door of the kitchen, he saw his old master leading the dancing with his group of friends. The boy found this so funny that he began to play faster and faster. The master and his friends soon got tired of dancing and tried to stop, but they couldn't. The sound of the violin kept making them dance, and they couldn't stop, no matter how hard they tried.

The boy came out of the kitchen with his violin and told his master, "I will stop playing when you pay me the wages you owe me."

The master was about to collapse from exhaustion, and he was willing to promise anything to get the music to stop. He told the boy, "Yes, I will pay you. Just stop playing the music." The boy believed the master and stopped playing the violin. All the people collapsed right where they were dancing, and the owner of the inn rushed over to ask if everyone was okay.

The master pushed himself up and bellowed, "I am not okay! That boy tried to kill me. Call the sheriff and have him arrested."

The master was so powerful that the owner of the inn immediately did what the master ordered. The sheriff came, arrested the boy, and took him to jail. He warned the boy not to try to escape and told him his trial would be in the morning.

The next morning the judge opened the trial of the boy. The master had come to give testimony that the boy had tried to kill him. When everyone heard the master's testimony, they knew that the boy must be convicted. The judge ended the trial early and sentenced the boy to prison and a life of hard labor. The little boy wondered if the Virgin was still watching over him, but he kept his faith and knew that in the end things would turn out for the best.

He asked the judge for one last request. "Before I am sent to jail, could I have my little violin to play just one more time?" The judge knew that the boy had been convicted only because of the power of the master, and he felt sorry for the boy, so he said yes.

The master tried to jump up and tell the judge not to say yes, but it was too late. The little boy had started playing.

Soon everyone in the courtroom was dancing. The more the boy played, the more they danced. Everyone was begging the boy to stop.

The boy shouted, "I'll stop playing as soon as the master tells the truth!"

By this time the master really was afraid he might die if the music didn't stop. He finally told everybody, "Yes, I promised him his wages and then I didn't pay him, but now I'll pay him double if he'll stop playing that horrible violin!"

The little boy stopped playing the violin. All the people in the court fell in their places, trying to catch their breath. Some even said, "I really liked that music. It just went on too long."

The master tried to escape out the door, but the sheriff stopped him. The judge had heard the master's confession and was going to hold him to his word. Before he left the courtroom, the master paid the boy double his wages.

The boy took his belongings and his little violin and went out into the world to seek his fortune, knowing that the Virgin was watching over him.

Taken from "The Magic Violin" in The Corn Woman Stories and Legends of the Hispanic Southwest *by Angel Vigil (Englewood, CO: Libraries Unlimited, 1994).*

Another version of the devil and the violin theme concerns a special fiddle and a frustrated would-be-musician in this Irish legend.

The One-Stringed Fiddle

(Ireland)

TREES WERE SACRED according to many people, and in Ireland the most sacred tree was the double-rooted brier tree. If one wished to gain magic powers, that person had to go to the double-rooted brier tree on the morning of May Day or November Day, just as the day was dawning. Then the person had to strip naked, crawl under the brier roots, and ask for the gift of magical powers.

Well, one Rake O'Neil was a mighty frustrated man. He loved music, and his greatest wish was to be able to play music. There was the problem. He could not learn one single note of music, even though he tried to learn all sorts of instruments. Being Irish, he first tried the Irish harp, but he was so bad that even the strings rebelled and snapped. Then he tried to play the flute, but the flute suffered until it warped into a twisted shape so that air was unable to pass through it. The same things happened when Rake tried to play the drums or any other instrument he could find.

The desire to make music grew so great that Rake went to the double-rooted brier on a November Day morning. A cold November morning it was, too, but he stripped naked and crawled on the frosty earth under the brier until he came out on the other side. While he was crawling, all he could think to say was, "I want the gift of music, I want the gift of music, I want the gift of music."

Shivering, Rake went to his pile of clothes to get dressed and there on top of them he found a queer-looking fiddle. It had only one string and seemed to call to him. Without even taking the time to put on his clothes, he picked up the fiddle and bow and tried it. When he drew the bow over the string, the miracle he wished for had happened. From the fiddle came the sweetest music he had ever heard.

He dressed swiftly and was delighted that he had his lifelong wish at last. From that morning onward, Rake was the star at every gathering, fair, party, and dance. When he played on his one-stringed fiddle, people were taken with his music and danced and sang along with it.

There was only one problem with Rake's music. The fiddle would play only one tune, but no one seemed to mind. Everyone enjoyed that one tune and declared that it was the finest music and that they could listen to it all day and all night, as people often did.

One day, at a particularly large fair on a bright sunny day, Rake was playing. A finely dressed foreign gentleman heard him and came over. This gentleman was buying horses for the king of France. He was so amazed by the music that he begged Rake to come with him and play for the king of France.

Rake was quite pleased with this request, so they took off together. Of course, the king and his court were enchanted with his music. Rake played the same tune every night at the court of the king of France for twenty years. Nobody grew tired of hearing him play; in fact they seemed more and more eager to hear it.

During all this time, no one else was able to play the one-stringed fiddle or to even learn its music, even though great musicians of France and Europe tried their best to do it.

Then it happened! One night, when it seemed like everyone in the French court except for the guards at the gates and their dogs was sleeping soundly, everyone woke up when a sound of music as loud as a clap of thunder pierced the quiet night. People's ears were ringing after the sound.

When everyone came back to their senses, they searched the palace to see what had caused the noise. They found Rake O'Neil dead in his bed. He always hung the fiddle over his bed at night, and there it was, broken into tiny shards and pieces on the floor.

It is still a mystery to this very day. Why had both Rake and the fiddle ceased to exist at that exact moment? Where did the music that everyone had heard come from? Maybe Rake and the one-stringed fiddle are still playing their same old tune somewhere out there.

There are many stories about the powers of the fiddle, most of them magical in one way or another.

The Magic Fiddle

(Byelorussia)*

ONCE UPON A TIME there lived a boy who in his earliest years began playing on a pipe. While tending bullocks, he would cut himself a reed, make a pipe out of it, and begin to play. The bullocks would stop nibbling the grass, prick up their ears, and listen. Hearing him, the birds in the forest would grow quiet, and even the frogs in the swamps would stop croaking.

He would go off to tend the horses at night, and it would be all gay and merry in the meadows, with the lads and lasses singing and joking, as young people should. The night would be beautiful and warm, and the ground fairly steaming.

And the boy would up and start playing on his pipe, and all the lads and lasses would grow quiet at once. And to each it seemed that a kind of balm had soothed the aching heart, and that an unknown force was raising him up and up to the bright stars in the deep blue sky.

The night herdsmen would sit there without stirring, forgetful of their aching, weary limbs and empty stomachs. They would sit there and listen.

And each felt he could spend a whole lifetime sitting on and on and listening to the enchanting melody.

The music would stop but no one dared so much as move from his place lest he frighten away the magical voice that poured out songs like the nightingale through the groves and forests and far into the sky.

Then the pipe would play again, a sorrowful tune this time, and sadness and melancholy would descend on all. Peasant men and

84

women, on their way late at night from their master's fields, would stop and listen on hearing it, and they never seemed to have their fill. Their lives would rise before their eyes, the poverty and the suffering, the cruel lord and the judge and stewards. And their hearts would be so heavy that they longed to give voice to their sadness in loud lamentations as they would have done for a dear departed soul, or for a son sent off to the wars.

But the sad tune would change to a gay one, and the listeners would throw down their scythes, rakes, and pitchforks, and with arms akimbo begin to dance.

The men and women, the horses, the trees, the stars, and clouds in the sky would dance—all the world would dance and make merry.

So great was the piper's magic power that he could do with the heart whatever he wished.

When he grew to manhood, the piper made himself a fiddle and with it roamed the land. Wherever he went, he would play his fiddle; and he dined and wined and was treated as the most welcome of guests and had good things heaped on him when he went on his way.

For many a long day the fiddler wandered over the land, a joy to good folk, a plague to cruel lords. A thorn in the side was he to the masters, for wherever he went, the bondsmen no longer obeyed their lords.

So the lords decided to do away with him, and first one, then another man did they try to send forth to kill or drown the fiddler. But no one was willing, for the peasants loved the fiddler, and the stewards thought him a sorcerer and were afraid.

Then the lords called up the demons from the netherworld, and together they plotted against him. For, of course, everyone knows that lords and demons are tarred with the same brush.

One day, when the fiddler was walking in the forest, the demons sent twelve hungry wolves against him. The wolves stood in the fiddler's path. They gnashed their teeth and their eyes gleamed like coals. And the fiddler had no weapon in his hand save the bag with his fiddle in it.

"My end has come," thought he.

So he took his fiddle from the bag, for he wished to make music just once more before dying. He leaned against a tree and drew his bow across the strings.

The fiddle spoke out like a living thing, and peals of music resounded in the forest. The bushes and trees became suddenly stilled, not a single leaf stirred; the wolves, jaws gaping, their hunger forgotten, stood frozen to the spot, listening intently.

And when the music stopped, the wolves moved off as in a dream to the depths of the forest.

The fiddler walked on. The sun was setting beyond the forest, its golden rays flecking the tops of the trees. It was so quiet that not a breath of sound could be heard.

The fiddler sat down on a riverbank, took out his fiddle, and began to play. So well did he play that earth and sky gave ear to him, seeming ready to listen forever. Then he struck up a gay polka, and all around began to dance: the stars whirled and twisted like the blizzard snow in winter, the clouds floated across the sky, and the fish leapt up and thrashed about until the river seethed like boiling water.

Even the king of the water sprites lost control and joined the dancing too, and such capers did he cut that the river overflowed its banks.

The demons were frightened and bounded out of their backwaters, but though they gnashed their teeth in fury, there was nothing they could do to the fiddler.

And the fiddler, seeing that the king of the water sprites was flooding the people's fields and gardens, stopped playing, put the fiddle into his bag, and went on his way.

He walked and he walked, and all of a sudden two young lords ran up to him.

"We have a ball tonight," said they. "Come and play for us, fiddler, and we shall pay you well."

The fiddler thought it over and what was he to do! The night was dark and he had nowhere to sleep and no money, either.

"Very well," said he, "I'll play for you."

The young lords brought the fiddler to a palace where there were so many young lords and ladies that there was no counting them.

Now on the table stood a large bowl, and one by one the lords and ladies were continually running to it. Each in turn thrust a finger into the bowl and then passed it across his eyes.

The fiddler, too, went up to the bowl, dipped in his finger, and passed it across his eyes. No sooner had he done so than he saw that this was no palace at all, but the netherworld itself, and these were no lords and ladies, but devils and witches.

"Oh, so that's the kind of ball it is!" said the fiddler to himself. "But just you wait, I'll play you a fine tune!"

So he turned up his fiddle and his bow struck its living strings, and all around him was shattered to dust. The devils and witches were scattered afar and were never seen again!

Taken from Folk Tales from Russian Lands, *selected and translated by Irina Zheleznova (New York: Dover Publications, 1969).*

Trouble starts for a fiddler when he tumbles out of this world and has to outwit a devil to get back.

The Russian Fiddler in Hell

(Russia)

A LONG TIME AGO IN RUSSIA, there was a peasant who had three sons. He lived quite well; in fact, he was rich. He became quite greedy. He collected two pots full of money about which he gloated to himself. He buried one in the threshing barn and the other under the gate. When he died, no one knew about the pots of money, because he had never told anyone.

One day there was a holiday celebration in the village and a fiddler was walking about leisurely enjoying himself. He suddenly fell through the ground and found himself in hell right at the very spot where the rich peasant was being tormented.

"Good day, good man," said the fiddler.

"You have landed in hell," said the peasant. "This is hell and we both are in it."

The fiddler asked him, "But good uncle, why were you sent here?"

"I was very greedy. It is all because of my money. I had a great deal of it, in fact two pots full, but I never gave to the poor. I buried the pots in the ground and never told anyone about them," answered the peasant. "Now I am doomed to be tormented, struck with sticks, and lacerated with claws."

The fiddler felt fear. "What should I do? I might be tormented, too!" he cried.

The answer from the peasant was, "Sit on the stove behind the chimney, do not eat for three years. That is how you can be saved."

Swiftly the fiddler hid behind the chimney. The devils returned to begin to beat the rich peasant. As they beat him they screeched, "That's for you, rich man! You hoarded a great deal of money. You

88

have made trouble for us. You buried it in places that give us a hard time guarding it. People and animals are constantly coming and going through the gate. Horses and cattle crush our heads with their hoofs. In the threshing barn we are continuously flailed and thrashed."

After the devils left, the weary peasant told the fiddler, "If you ever get out of here, tell my children to get the money. One pot of money is buried under the gate and the other pot is buried in the threshing barn. Tell my children to give it all to the poor."

Shortly a whole band of devils came rushing in. They stopped and sniffed the air. "Why is there a Russian smell here?" they asked.

"Maybe it is because you have just been to Russia and you still have the Russian smell in your noses," offered the peasant.

"That's impossible!" All the devils began to search and kept following their noses until they found the fiddler hiding behind the chimney. "Ha, ha, ha, haaaa!" they screamed. "A fiddler is in here." They dragged him down from the stove and forced him to play his fiddle.

The poor fiddler played for three years, but amazingly it seemed like three days to him. "How strange! Sometimes I played and tore all of my strings in one evening and now I've played for three years and not one string has broken. How amazing!"

No sooner had he thought this than all of his strings snapped. "Well, devils, you can see for yourselves that my strings have broken. I have nothing to play on," said the fiddler.

One of the devils jumped into the air and said, "Wait! I have two sets of strings and I'll get them for you." He jumped, skipped, and ran away and was back quickly with more strings.

The fiddler took them, strung them on his fiddle, and tightened them. The first set of strings snapped. He strung and tightened the second set and they too snapped. "No, devils. I cannot use your strings. There's another way out of this. I have some more strings at home. If you let me go, I'll bring them back here."

"You won't come back," yelled the devils in a chorus.

"Well, if you don't trust me, send one of your devils to go back with me," suggested the fiddler. The devils chose one of their company to go with the fiddler.

The fiddler returned to his village and heard the bells ringing for a wedding. The wedding was being celebrated in the last house on the street. "Let's go to that wedding!" he said.

"Let's," answered the devil.

They went into the house. Everyone recognized the fiddler and asked him, "Where have you been for three years? We have missed you!"

"I have been in hell," replied the fiddler. Everyone laughed uproariously.

"We must go now," said the devil.

"Wait a little while. Let me play my fiddle and amuse the young couple and their guests," begged the fiddler.

And so he played there until the cocks began to crow to greet the morning sun. The devil vanished, poof!

The fiddler told the rich peasant's sons, who were at the wedding, "Your father orders you to take his money and give it all to the poor. One pot is buried under the gate and another in the threshing barn. He said to be sure and give it all to the poor."

The peasant's sons dug up the money and began to distribute it to the poor, but the more they gave, the more there was in the pots. They put the pots in the middle of the crossroads. Everyone who passed by took out as many coins as they could clutch, and still the money did not decrease.

A petition was sent to the tsar saying that in a certain village there was a winding road and that a straight road would shorten the distance traveled considerably. The tsar gave orders that a straight bridge be built. A bridge was erected and this used up all of the money from the two pots.

At this very same time, a maiden gave birth to a son and abandoned him. This baby boy did not eat or drink for three years and when the boy came to the bridge he said, "Oh, what a wonderful bridge! Wouldn't it be nice if the person who built it would be rewarded?"

The angels in heaven heard his prayer and told the Lord. He ordered his angels to release the rich peasant from the darkness of hell. The peasant was grateful to the fiddler for the rest of his happy life.

Remember that one definition for a legend is a lie that has attained the dignity of age.

The Legend of the Fiddler of High Lonesome

(United States)

N A MOUNTAIN IN COLORADO, above 10,000 feet in elevation, where the mountain breezes constantly blow and wet, fat snowflakes can pile up in June, is a ten-foot monument to a man who was and is a legend. A poignant legend.

Clifford Griffin came to the west from his home in England in the late 1800s. He was born July 2, 1847, to a successful lawyer and his elegant wife, but was inclined to the arts. His younger brother, Heneage, who had come west earlier, had invested in some mining property. Heneage brought Clifford to America to work with him. Clifford had been unable to find direction for his life while living on the family estates. Tragedy had been a too-often visitor to his life. His beloved mother had gone insane and died, and several brothers and sisters had died while very young, and Clifford seemed adrift.

Maybe Heneage brought Clifford to the frontier when he found out that Clifford's fiancee had been found dead in Clifford's room the night before they were to be married. No one ever was able to discover any of the details—it remained a mystery.

Clifford had a cabin high on the mountain by the 7:30 mine. They called the mine the 7:30 because the miners were called to work at 7:30 rather than the traditional 6:30 start.

It was Clifford's habit to sit on a huge outcrop in the evening to watch the beauty of the sunset, listen to the hummingbirds as they whirred by, and play his violin. His music could be heard throughout the valley and in the mining town of Silver Plume below. Some evenings the music was bright and catchy, sometimes it was serene, but many times it was melancholy.

Clifford frequented the saloons in the town below and there he drank and also played his violin for the customers. Everyone found pleasure in his company, even though they didn't know anything about him personally. He was a handsome, well-built man with dark hair, a mustache, and dancing eyes. He was pleasant, cultured, and seemed to have an air of mystery about him.

Up on the mountain near his cabin, Clifford blasted a huge opening in the solid rock. He had asked his brother to bury him there when he died. The miners went by this spot every morning on their way to the mine.

In the spring of 1887, Clifford's evening concerts from atop his perch on his rock became longer and full of sadness. People listening from their porches down in Silver Plume enjoyed these concerts, but detected the sorrow in the music. That was the way things went until the evening of June 19, 1887. That night the fiddler of high lonesome played like he had never played before. The mountain breezes carried melody after melody to the listeners. Then the music stopped. Not much later there was the sound of a single gunshot.

People, fearing the worst, hurried up to Clifford's cabin and there they found him. He had shot himself and fallen down into the opening he had blasted in the rock. There he lay on his back. He looked at peace.

The evenings of music were over for the townsfolk. Heneage erected a ten-foot monument on the rocky outcrop where Clifford was buried and then moved away and was never heard of again.

Come to Colorado sometimes and travel to Silver Plume on Interstate 70 west of Denver. Drive into the small town and park your car at the base of the mountain. Lower the car windows and feel the breeze on your face, listen for the hummingbirds, and maybe, just maybe, you will hear the strains of a violin on the winds. Some say Clifford can be heard when everything is just right, playing a love song.

In many areas there has been made a connection between the guitar, witches, and devils.

The Legend of the Tuscany Guitar

(Italy)

 TRAVELER THROUGH ITALY came to Tuscany, where the grapes were rich and the women sweet. The traveler, named Antonio, had taken his inheritance from a rich uncle and used it to travel. His one ambition was to travel all over Italy and Greece. While in the small town of Tuscany, he met a special woman named La Magdalena, who had raven-black hair and eyes that looked old and bright at the same time. They met in a cafe and took an immediate liking to each other. At first they flirted with each other and sang songs with the strolling musicians in the town.

As they got to know each other, they shared their life stories—somewhat. Antonio told La Magdalena all about his large musical family. His father sang opera in their little village as he cooked delicious food in his restaurant. People came from miles around to eat his food and hear his singing. Antonio also told her about his mother, sisters, and brothers. There were even stories about the family pet, who also sang, or so it seemed.

All of La Magdalena's stories seemed to center around the past few years. There were no childhood memories, there seemed to be no family, and yet she told Antonio stories that seemed to be mysterious. And always, they sang as they walked holding hands, sitting on benches by the river, or hiding from the sun under a fig tree.

La Magdalena knew songs he had never heard. One of her songs was about a witch also named La Magdalena. When she would finish singing it, she would grow quiet, and yet she sang it frequently.

After some time, Antonio asked La Magdalena to marry him. "I can't" was all that she would say. She wouldn't even give him a reason, just, "I can't."

The more he asked her, the more upset she became until one evening with a large, bright full moon, La Magdalena whispered her story to him.

"This will probably be the end of our love, for love you I truly do. There are reasons, though, why I can't marry you. Now I will tell them to you. Only please do not think the less of me for what I am going to tell you."

"I am not as young as you think I am. In fact I am older than you can imagine," she confided.

Antonio just tossed his head and laughed. "Oh, now I get it! You are worried about something as little as being older than me."

"Dear Antonio, I am not just a little bit older than you. And that isn't all. It all began more than a hundred years ago ..."

That was all that Antonio let her say. "Old family stories don't worry me either."

La Magdalena looked him in his eyes. "There is so much to tell you! More than one hundred years ago, I lived in a town up north, but life was not simple. You see, I was a witch. I loved to dance and sing and make music. People weren't afraid of me except for one other witch, who was jealous of me. She worked her magic and turned me into a guitar."

Antonio had become quiet and serious at this point, because he could see that she was telling him her real story at last.

"I was a guitar with a rich tone and everyone who played me fell in love with me. I belonged to a minstrel, a Gypsy, a concert musician, a musician in the king's court, and many others. Always, my music was the richest ever heard. Then a wizard musician heard my music one day and knew that I was no ordinary instrument. He stole me from my owner and made a fortune with my music. When he was old and near death, he restored me to my human likeness and gave me my freedom. I had to spend one hundred years as a guitar before I could be freed. It was a long century, but also a century full of magical music. There you have my story and now you know why I cannot marry you."

La Magdalena was right. They never married because she disappeared mysteriously after that. Legends tell, though, of haunting guitar music coming from near the river and from under a certain fig tree.

This is the story of how music helped a famous musician and poet to escape from the clutches of pirates.

Arion and His Harp

(Greece)

N THE COURT OF PERIANDER, king of Corinth, dwelt Arion, the greatest singer of tales. Arion was a great favorite of Periander.

"There is to be a musical contest in Sicily and I want to compete for the prize," Arion told Periander.

"Stay with me. Be contented. He who strives to win in contests of all kinds may lose," advised Periander. "Besides, I want you to stay here with me."

"A wandering life is happiness for a bard. I want to share my talents and joys with others," said Arion. "Besides, if I win the prize, my fame will be increased along with my pleasure at winning."

Arion left Corinth for Sicily where he was undisputed winner of the contest. After a day of celebration, he left for Corinth on a Corinthian ship with his chest full of newly won riches and rewards. He was eager to share his victory and riches with his friend Periander.

The waters were calm, the breezes gentle, and the sky cloudless. It wasn't the travel that was to prove dangerous. That came from the greed of men. Arion had taken a stroll on the deck, and he overheard the seamen plotting to kill him for his riches. There was nowhere to go to escape. When the crew approached him with, "Arion, you must die! If you want to be buried onshore, surrender to us and die on this spot. Otherwise, throw yourself into the sea," they yelled.

"Take my gold if that is what you want, but spare my life," argued Arion.

"No! You must die. Alive you would tell Periander, and we would never be able to escape from him. You must die!" they decreed.

"Then you must grant me one last wish," he asked. "If I must die, I would like to die as I have lived, as a bard with my death song and my harp strings winging their way in the breezes. Then I will bid farewell to life and go to my fate."

Even these pirates were eager to hear such a famous musician, and they agreed. Even the rude and crude admire beauty.

"I must dress in proper clothes for such a performance," Arion said. "Apollo would be disappointed to meet me unless I was clad in my minstrel raiments." With this he dressed himself in his gold and purple tunic with graceful billows, his jewels on his arms, a golden wreath on his fair head, and exquisite perfume. He held his lyre in his left hand and struck it with an ivory wand. Arion appeared to be inspired as he smelled the morning air and admired the glittering morning rays.

The seamen were entranced as Arion went to stand on the side of the vessel. He looked down into the deep blue sea and began to sing. He sang of his new life among the gods and wise ones. As the last notes of his harp strings vibrated in the air, he turned and leapt off the boat. His tunic floated like wings in the air. He soon was covered by the waves and gone from sight.

The evil crew felt safe and continued on their way to Corinth, feeling secure that their crime would not be detected.

What the crewmen did not know was that Arion's music had enchanted the inhabitants of the deep to come closer to listen, and that dolphins followed the ship as if chained by a spell. As Arion started to float toward the surface of the water, a dolphin offered him his back. Arion mounted the dolphin, which carried him safely to shore.

At the spot on the rocky shore where Arion landed, there was later erected a monument of brass to preserve the memory of this amazing event.

After bidding farewell to the dolphin, Arion started his trip on foot to Corinth. He played and sang as he went, quite full of love and happiness. When he entered the halls of Periander, he was grateful for what he had—life and music. He told Periander what had happened and Periander ordered him to stay hidden so that when the evildoers came to report on their arrival, they would do so not knowing that Arion had been saved.

When the ship arrived in the harbor, Periander summoned the mariners before him. "Have you heard anything of my beloved friend Arion?" he asked them. "I am quite anxious for his return."

"We left him well and prosperous in Tarentum," they said. Just as they said that, Arion stepped forth and faced them. The criminals fell prostrate at his feet and cried, "We meant to kill you but you have returned as a god."

"He lives," said Periander. "He lives, the master of music. Kind heaven protects men such as him. You greedy murderers are lucky that Arion does not seek revenge. Be gone with you all. May your lives never experience the sights and sounds of beauty again."

Arion had many more years left to him to create celestial music and sing the praises of the dolphins.

In ancient Greece, music, poetry, prophecy, and healing were not clearly distinguished from another. Poets of old spoke of the healing power of song. This magical power was a result of both the music and the words.

Orpheus and Eurydice

(Greece)

THE GREATEST MORTAL MUSICIAN was Orpheus, the son of Apollo and Calliope, the Muse of epic poetry.

Orpheus played on his lyre and sang songs of such beauty that nature itself was enchanted. Nothing could withstand the charm of his perfect music. It was not unusual, while he played and sang, to see rocks move closer to hear him. These very rocks relaxed and softened under the charm of his music. Trees also crowded in to hear Orpheus's serenade. It has even been said that the moon and sun rested on the branches of an oak tree as he played. Listening frogs were very slow and careful as they came from below the earth's crust to join the audience. Fierce wild beasts stood entranced alongside creatures that usually became their meals. All was peace and quiet joy when Orpheus caressed the strings of the lyre with his ivory wand.

Orpheus fell deeply in love with the nymph Eurydice, who also was under the spell of him and his music. Of course, he courted her with his songs of love and devotion, and soon they were married.

Such a happy, peaceful life they lived! That is, until the day Eurydice went wandering with her friends, the nymphs, in a meadow filled with swaying wildflowers. Aristaeus, a shepherd, saw her and was dazzled by her beauty and grace. He immediately made bold advances to her and she fled from him. As she dashed off, she stepped upon a snake in the grass and was bitten on her foot. No one was able to save her from death from this bite.

Orpheus was overcome with grief. He sang of this tragic death to all who would listen, but his songs only made those who heard them sad and choked with tears. Orpheus decided that he must take action and descended to the region of the dead. There his songs of lament for Eurydice were so beautiful that even Cerberus, the three-headed guard dog of the underworld, was charmed and let him pass. Orpheus passed through crowds of ghosts and moved the king and queen of the dead with his music and words of sorrow. He pleaded for the life of Eurydice and argued that she had died too soon. If they would not grant her return to Orpheus, he himself would surely die and stay in the land of the dead. His tender strains moved the ghosts themselves to tears. Thirsty Tantalus stopped his efforts for water, the great wheel stood still, the vulture stopped tearing at Prometheus's liver, the daughters of Danaus rested from their task of drawing water in a sieve, and Sisyphus, the dead king of Corinth who had been condemned to perpetually roll a big rock uphill, which when it reached the top, rolled down again, sat on his rock to listen.

Orpheus's eloquent music touched the king and queen of the dead and they allowed Eurydice to return to life on earth with Orpheus. There was only one condition: Orpheus must not look at her before reaching the entrance of the underworld.

Eurydice, who limped on her wounded foot, was helped by Orpheus as they traveled back to earth. They traveled through narrow, dark, steep passages. Finally they saw faint rays from the light of the world and Orpheus, in a moment of joyful forgetfulness, cast a glance at Eurydice and she instantly disappeared, returning to the underworld forever. They instinctively stretched out their arms to embrace each other but clutched only air.

Orpheus tried to follow her and begged for permission to return, but the stern ferryman refused to help him further. He stayed on the banks of the river for seven days without food or sleep. From then on his sorrow was boundless. He sang his complaints to the rocks and mountains, tigers and oaks. He refused all advances made to him by other women and continued to lament his loss with song.

Some Thracian women became so angry at his lack of interest in them that they tore him to pieces in a frenzy. Even then, as they threw his head and lyre into the river, the head of Orpheus and his lyre continued to bring forth their beautiful music. The Muses gathered up the fragments of his body and buried them where the nightingale is said to sing over his grave more sweetly than in any other part of Greece. Jupiter placed his lyre among the stars.

The spirit of Orpheus returned to the underworld of the dead where the lovers once again found each other and where they now roam the happy fields together.

Part Three
Suggestions for Extending Experiences

♪ Research a variety of stringed instruments: violin, viola, cello, bass, and others. How is a guitar, harp, or banjo different? Bring in a player of a stringed instrument to demonstrate and discuss the instruments.

♪ Share Marguerite W. Davol's *The Heart of the Wood* (New York: Simon & Schuster, 1992), which describes the making of a violin. Invite a violin maker to share the art of instrument making.

♪ Build your own original instrument. Possible materials for use in making stringed instruments include: cigar boxes, rubber bands, tubes, straws, cans, boxes, pieces of wood, beans, wooden spoons, pie pans, paper towel rolls, grass, and string.

♪ Start a file collection of newspaper and magazine articles related to stringed instruments. Review them after a selected period of time and develop a chart that shows how they are alike and how they are different. Consult a librarian for articles in this file.

♪ Find recordings of expressive string music, such as Beethoven's "Romances" for violin. Practice reading one of these stories, such as "Orpheus and Eurydice," with the music in the background.

♪ Illustrate one of the stories in this section. Some possible forms for illustration include collage, stitchery, oil paint, chalk, clay sculptures, crayons, and watercolors.

♪ Bring in a map of Greece. Find all the sites mentioned in "Arion and His Harp." Where might "Orpheus and Eurydice" take place?

♪ Rewrite one of the stories for a choral reading presentation.

♪ Find recordings that feature the violin, lute, harp, guitar, lyre, or any other stringed instrument. Listen to some of this music and share your reactions with others.

♪ Find all the countries from this section of stories using stringed instruments. Place sticky notes with the title of the story and the instrument on a map of the appropriate country.

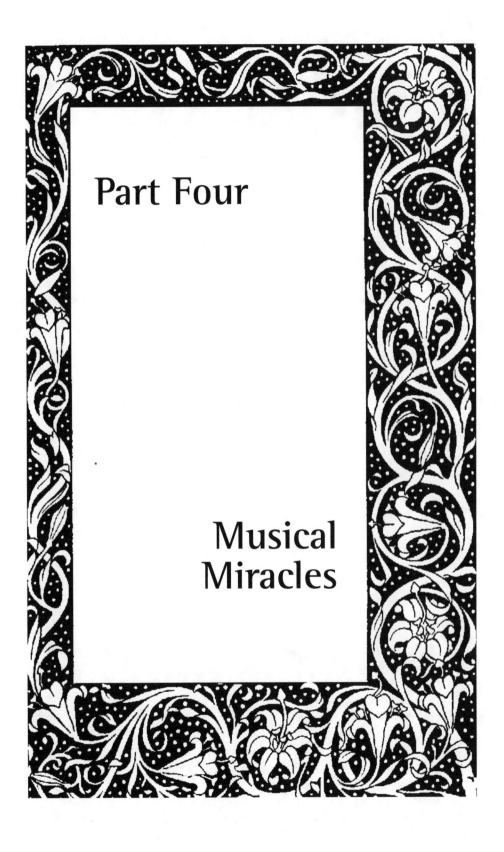

Part Four

Musical Miracles

This is the story of a murder mystery and how a singing bone's message solved the crime.

The Singing Bone

(Germany)*

 WILD BOAR TERRORIZED a certain country; it attacked workers in the fields, killed men, and tore them to pieces with its terrible tusks. The king of the country had offered rich rewards to anyone who would rid the land of this monster, but no man could even be persuaded to enter the forest where the animal made its home, because the beast was so huge and ferocious.

In desperation the king proclaimed that he would give his only daughter in marriage to the man who would bring the wild boar to him dead or alive.

Two brothers lived in this country. They were the sons of a poor man. They gave notice that they would enter into this perilous undertaking. The elder, who was clever and crafty, was influenced by pride. The younger brother was innocent and simple and offered himself from the kindness of his heart.

The king advised them that the best and safest way would be to take opposite directions in the wood. The elder brother was to go in the evening, the younger in the morning.

The younger brother had not gone far when a little fairy stepped up to him. The fairy held in his hand a black spear and said, "I will give you this spear, because your heart is innocent and good. With this you can go out and discover the wild boar, and he shall not be able to harm you."

The younger brother thanked the little man, took the spear, placed it on his shoulder, and without delay went farther into the forest. It was not long before he saw the animal coming toward him all ready to spring on him. The youth stood still and held the spear firmly in front of him. In a wild rage, the fierce beast ran violently toward him and was met by the spear. It seemed that the boar threw himself on the point, and as it pierced his heart, the animal fell dead.

The younger brother took the dead monster on his shoulder and set off to find his brother. As he approached the other side of the wood, he saw a large hall and heard music. He found a number of people dancing, drinking wine, and making merry. His elder brother was among them, because he wished to gather up his courage for the evening with cheerful company and wine.

When the older brother caught sight of the youth coming out of the forest laden with the boar, jealousy and malice rose in his heart. He disguised his bitter feelings and spoke kindly to his brother, "Come in and stay with us, dear brother, and rest a while. Get up your strength by a cup of wine."

Not suspecting that anything was wrong, the younger brother carried the dead boar into the hall. He told his brother of the little man he had met in the wood who had given him the spear. He described, too, how he had killed the vicious animal.

The older brother persuaded him to stay and rest till the evening, and then they went out together in the twilight and walked by the river till the night became quite dark. A little bridge lay across the river that they had to pass. The elder brother let the young one go before him. In the middle of the stream, the wicked man gave his younger brother a blow from behind, and the youth fell down dead instantly.

Fearing the youth might not be quite dead, the older brother threw the body over the bridge into the river. Through the clear waters he saw it sink into the sand. After this wicked deed, he took the dead wild boar on his shoulders, ran home, and carried it to the king. He pretended that he had killed the animal, and, therefore, he claimed the princess as his wife according to the king's promise.

But dark deeds are not often concealed, for something usually happens to bring them to light. And so it was that not many years after, a herdsman passing over the bridge with his flock saw beneath him in the sand a little bone as white as snow. He thought it would make a nice mouthpiece for his horn. So as soon as the flock passed over the bridge, he waded into the middle of the stream—for the water was very shallow—took up the bone, and carried it home.

He made a mouthpiece for his horn, but the first time he blew the horn, the herdsman was filled with wonder and amazement, for it began to sing. These were the words it sang:

> Ah! dear shepherd, you are blowing your horn
> With one of my bones, which night and morn
> Lie still unburied, beneath the wave
> Where I was thrown in a sandy grave.
> I killed the wild boar, and my brother slew me,
> And gained the princess by pretending 'twas he.

"What a wonderful horn," said the shepherd. "It can sing of itself! I must certainly take it to my lord, the king."

When the horn was brought before the king and blown by the shepherd, it at once began to sing the same song with the same words. The king at first was surprised, but his suspicion was aroused. He ordered the sand under the bridge to be examined immediately. The entire skeleton of the murdered man was discovered, and the whole ghastly deed came to light.

The wicked brother could not deny the deed, however. And the king ordered him to be tied in a sack and drowned. But the remains of his murdered brother were carefully carried to the churchyard and laid to rest in a beautiful grave.

Collected by Jacob Grimm and Wilhelm Grimm.

There are all sorts of variants on this African-American folk story.

The Singing Bones
(United States)

ONCE UPON A TIME there lived a man and a woman. The man's first wife had died and his new wife was a widow. Between them they had twenty-five children, and they were very poor. The man was a good man, but his wife was bad. Every day when the husband returned from his work, his wife served him dinner, but always the dinner was meat without bones.

"Why does this meat have no bones?" he asked her.

"Because bones are heavy and meat is cheaper without the bones. They give more for the money," was her reply.

"You fix dinners of meat with no bones, so why is it that you don't eat meat?" he asked.

"Ha, you forget that I have lost all of my teeth. How do you think I could eat meat with no teeth?" she answered.

"Yes, yes, that is a fact," mused the husband. He said nothing more because he was afraid to upset his wife, who was as wicked as she was ugly. There was something else that was strange. He seemed to hear voices singing outside his house, but he never found anyone out there singing.

When one has twenty-five children, one cannot think of them all the time. If one or two are missing, you don't notice it right away. One day after his dinner, the husband asked for his children. When they were by him he counted them and found only fifteen. "Wife, where are our ten other children?" he asked.

"They are at their grandmother's. Every day I send one more to get a change of air and scenery," she told him. That was certainly true, because every day there was one more child missing.

106

One day the man came home from work. He stood at the threshold of his house in front of a large stone that was there. He was thinking of his children and how he wanted to go and get them at their grandmother's. Suddenly he heard voices singing:

> Mother killed us,
> Father ate us,
> We are not in a coffin,
> We are not buried in the cemetery.

At first the startled father did not understand what that meant. He looked under the stone and there found a great quantity of bones. The bones began to sing again. They sang the same song. Then the man understood that these were the bones of the missing children, and that his wife had killed them, and he had eaten them. He became so angry that he killed his wicked wife. He then buried the children's bones in the cemetery and stayed alone at his house. From that time on, he never ate meat because he remembered what meat he had eaten before.

Musical instruments have been used also as instruments for destruction.

Joshua and the Battle of Jericho

(Israel)

FTER THE DEATH OF MOSES, Joshua the son of Nun, Moses' minister, was selected by the Lord to lead the people. The Lord caused the waters of the River Jordan to dry so the children of Israel could cross safely on their journey of escape.

The city of Jericho was closed to Joshua's people, so the Lord's host told Joshua to "surround the city with men of war and circle it and go around it for six days. Seven priests shall bear before the ark of the covenant seven trumpets of rams' horns. On the seventh day, circle the city of Jericho one more time, and the priests shall blow with the trumpets."

Joshua was further instructed that when the priests made a long blast with the rams' horns, all the people should shout with a great shout when they heard the sound of the trumpets. The Lord's host told Joshua that the wall of the city would fall down flat and the people could go forward.

Joshua called the priests and told them to take up the ark of the covenant and let seven priests bear seven trumpets of rams' horns before the ark of the Lord. He told them to pass on and surround the city with the armed forces in front. And so it was.

Joshua told the people not to shout nor make any noise with their voices. They were not to speak until the day he bid them shout. Then they were to shout with all of their might.

And so the ark of the Lord surrounded the city and circled about it once. They came to a camp and camped there. Early the next morning, Joshua and the priests again took up the ark of the Lord and went on continuously blowing the trumpets for a second day. Again they returned to the camp. So it was for six days.

On the seventh day they rose about the dawning of the day, circled the city, and on that day they went around it for the seventh time.

This time, when the priests blew with the trumpets Joshua told the people to "shout, for the Lord hath given you the city."

So when the people heard the sound of the trumpets, they shouted with a great shout, and the wall did indeed fall down flat so that the people were able to go up into the city and take it.

That is the story of Joshua fighting the battle of Jericho.

A group of men from Scotland and their bagpipes combine to win a battle in India.

Jordy and the Ladies from Hell

(Canada)

AN OLD SCOTSMAN used to enjoy telling stories of war to a young listener in Canada. Jordy had fought with the English forces in the late 1800s in India. At that time, India was part of the British Empire, and local hill tribes were in revolt, so the English forces were sent to subdue them.

Jordy was among these soldiers. The English forces traditionally fought in a square formation. In this particular battle, the square was not the best way for the men to fight, and they were being overrun by the local forces. Jordy told his young friend that he had suffered several bullet wounds himself and he was one of the few left who was still able to fight.

The local tribesmen would hit and run, weakening the ranks of the English. Just when Jordy figured that the end was imminent, a wailing sound was heard coming toward them. As it got closer it became evident that new English forces were arriving and they were being led by a group of Scotch bagpipers dressed in their kilts. As the bagpipe skirls and wails were getting closer, the tribesmen ran in terror shouting, "Run, run! It is the ladies from hell."

And so Jordy's life was saved that day by the arrival of the Scotch Ladies from Hell, but several bullets remained lodged in his body as tokens of the battle. Jordy's young listener now knew why tears welled up in Jordy's eyes whenever he heard the music of the bagpipes.

Suggestions for Extending Experiences

♪ Find and collect other variants of the story "The Singing Bones." Ask a librarian for help if you need it. Make a bibliography of these variants. How are they alike and different?

♪ Write a poem that involves music in a dramatic conclusion. Create music to go with it. The Canadian Brass Quintet would be a good source of appropriate music.

♪ Beethoven's Ninth Symphony is his musical statement defying his deafness. Find someone to listen to a recording of this symphony with you and share your reactions to the music.

♪ If you were the coach of a competitive sport team, what music could you use to inspire them?

♪ Is there any music that has touched you or moved you emotionally? If so, what was it and why did it impress you?

♪ Conduct a survey to find out what music inspires people. Why did people choose the music they did? Compile the results of your study and share it with family or friends.

♪ Because research has discovered that listening to Mozart improved college student test scores, use this information to stimulate your intellectual endeavors. Get a copy of the compact disc or cassette "Mozart Makes You Smarter" (Sony Masterworks, MFK 66245) and listen to it before and during intellectual activities.

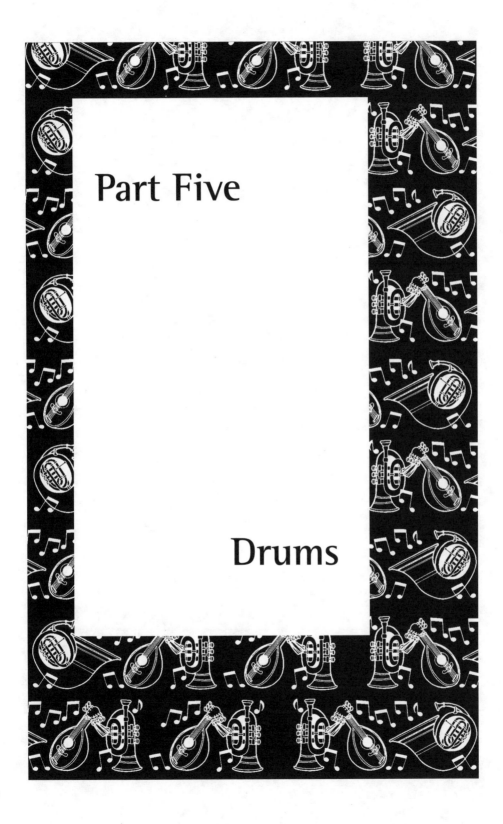

Part Five

Drums

Drums are among the most ancient and most sacred of all musical instruments. Many cultures respect the power of drums and the rhythms that reflect the steady beat of the heart and the cadences of running, walking, working, and playing.

Osebo's Drum

(Ghana)*

OSEBO, THE LEOPARD, once had a great drum which was admired by all animals and gods. Although everyone admired it, no one ever hoped to own it, for Osebo was then the most powerful of animals on earth, and he was feared. Only Nyame, the Sky God, had ambitions to get the drum from the leopard.

It happened that Nyame's mother died, and he began the preparations for a spectacular funeral. He wondered what he could do to make the ceremony worthy of the family. People said to him, "For this ceremony we need the great drum of Osebo."

And Nyame said, "Yes, I need the drum of Osebo."

But Nyame didn't know how he could get the drum. At last he called the earth animals before him, all but the leopard himself. Nyame's stool was brought out, and he sat upon it, while his servants held over his head the many-colored parasol which is called the rainbow. He said to the animals, "For the funeral ceremonies I need the great drum of the leopard. Who will get it for me?"

Esono, the elephant, said, "I will get it." He went to where the leopard lived and tried to take the drum, but the leopard drove him away. The elephant came back to the house of the Sky God, saying, "I could not get it."

Then Gyata, the lion, said, "I will get the drum." He went to the place of the leopard and tried to take the drum, but the leopard drove him off. And Gyata, the lion, returned to the house of the Sky God, saying, "I could not get it."

Adowa, the antelope, went, but he couldn't get it. Odenkyem, the crocodile, went, but he couldn't get it. Owea, the tree bear, went, but he couldn't get it. Many animals went, but the leopard drove them all away.

Then Akykyigie, the turtle, came forward. In those days the turtle had a soft back like other animals. He said to the Sky God, "I will get the drum."

When people heard this, they broke into a laugh, not even bothering to cover their mouths. "If the strong creatures could not get Osebo's drum," they said, "how will you, who are so pitifully small and weak?"

The turtle said, "No one else has been able to bring it. How can I look more foolish than the rest of you?"

And he went down from the Sky God's house, slowly, slowly, slowly, until he came to the place of the leopard. When Osebo saw him coming, he cried out, "Are you, too, a messenger from Nyame?"

The turtle replied, "No, I come out of curiosity. I want to see if it is true."

The leopard said, "What are you looking for?"

"Nyame, the Sky God, has built himself a great new drum," the turtle said. "It is so large that he can enter into it and be completely hidden. People say his drum is greater than yours."

Osebo answered, "There is no drum greater than mine."

Akykyigie, the turtle, looked at Osebo's drum, saying, "I see it, I see it, but it is not so large as Nyame's. Surely it isn't large enough to crawl into."

Osebo said angrily, "Why is it not large enough?" And to show the turtle, Osebo crawled into the drum.

The turtle said, "It is large indeed, but your hindquarters are showing."

The leopard squeezed further into the drum.

The turtle said, "Oh, but your tail is showing."

The leopard pulled himself further into the drum. Only the tip of his tail was out.

"Ah," the turtle said, "a little more and you will win!"

The leopard wriggled and pulled in the end of his tail.

Then the turtle plugged the opening of the drum with an iron cooking pot. And while the leopard cried out fiercely, the turtle tied the drum to himself and began dragging it slowly, slowly, slowly to the house of Nyame, the Sky God. He dragged for a while, then he stopped to beat the drum as a signal that he was coming.

When the animals heard the great drum of Osebo, they trembled in fear, for they thought surely it was Osebo himself who was playing. But when they saw the turtle coming, slowly, slowly, slowly, dragging the great drum behind him, they were amazed.

The turtle came before the Sky God and said, "Here is the drum. I have brought it. And inside the drum is Osebo himself. What shall I do with him?"

Inside the drum Osebo heard, and he feared for his life. He said, "Let me out, and I will go away in peace."

The turtle said, "Shall I kill him?"

The animals all said, "Yes, kill him."

But Osebo called out, "Do not kill me; allow me to go away. The drum is for the Sky God, and I won't complain."

So the turtle removed the iron pot which covered the opening in the drum. Osebo came out frightened. He came hurriedly. And he came out backward, tail first. Because he couldn't see where he was going, he fell into the Sky God's fire, and his hide was burned in many little places by the hot embers. He leaped from the fire and hurried away. But the marks of the fire, where he was burned, still remain, and that is why all leopards have dark spots.

The Sky God said to the turtle, "You have brought the great drum of Osebo to make music for the funeral of my mother. What can I give you in return?"

The turtle looked at all the other animals. He saw that they were jealous of his great deed. And he feared that they would try to abuse him for doing what they could not do. So he said to Nyame, "Of all things that could be, I want a hard cover the most."

So the Sky God gave the turtle a hard shell to wear on his back. And never is the turtle seen without it.

Taken from The Hat-Shaking Dance and Other Ashanti Tales from Ghana *by Harold Courlander and Albert Kofi Prempeh; illustrations by Enrico Arno (New York: Harcourt, Brace and World, 1957).*

The Bantu people of the Congo tell another story about the creation of the drum.

The Drum

(Congo)

IN THE DEEP DARKNESS of the tropical rain forest of the Congo, there lived a bird called Nchonzo nkila. It was a bird like other birds—wings, feathers, and such—but its tail was shaped like a round drum. Nchonzo discovered he had something special with his tail. Other creatures grew to respect the Nchonzo nkila because he went around beating his tail up and down on the earth creating a sound never heard before. Wherever he went, he amused himself by making this new sound.

The equator runs through the Congo, so it is hot and humid and its creatures like to take afternoon rests when the heat is at its worst. But how could bugs of the earth, little critters that live in the trees, or birds take a proper rest when Nchonzo nkila took this time to smack his tail and make his boom everywhere?

Ants would come to the hole of their anthills and beg Nchonzo nkila to be quiet as he banged his tail near them. Monkeys would swing from the trees to the earth beside him and, at first, politely ask him to be quiet. When he kept up his booming with his tail, they were no longer polite. "Shut up!" they would chatter to him. Lizards crawling through the bush would only hiss their unhappiness with his constant booming.

How proud Nchonzo nkila was to be the only one to make this wonderful rich sound. He persisted in making afternoon naps impossible for all. Then one day, even Nzambi, the Mother Earth, tired of his endless thumps on her. "I have certainly had enough of your ceaseless pounding on me. Give me that tail of yours so there can be some peace here," she demanded.

118

"Aha," said Nchonzo nkila. "Even you, Mother Earth, are jealous of my powers. No, I think I shall keep my tail and its wonderful sound."

All of the bugs, beasts, and birds of the forest heard this and they decided to ask Mother Earth to do something about this eternal noise. They each told her how they were unhappy with the lack of quiet when they wanted to slumber. "Not only that," said a small mouse, "when he beats his booming tail near my home, dirt falls off the walls and ceilings of my home, and then not only do I not get a rest, but I then have to clean up the mess he has made."

"Yes," said the beetle, "he mashes up all of the fresh dirt I have dug and pounds things down in other places with that wretched tail of his."

After listening to all of the creatures' complaints, Mother Earth again addressed Nchonzo nkila. "You are making all of the bugs, beasts, and birds unhappy with your wonderful talent." You see, this time Mother Earth thought she could win the battle with flattery. "How much more everyone would appreciate it if you would give us concerts just as evening brings the dusk to the forest. It would be so special that way."

"Ha, aha!" roared Nchonzo nkila. "With such talent as I have everyone and everything should be pleased that I choose to share my unique talents with all. I choose to do this when I feel it is the right time."

"All right, Nchonzo nkila," warned Mother Earth. "Maybe it will be the best thing to do if I take your tail away from you. Then we all can have some rest."

But even Mother Earth was not allowed to deprive the creator of the drum of its ownership. That is how the drum came to be invented and why Nchonzo nkila still plays it whenever he pleases.

Suggestions for Extending Experiences

♪ Experiment with percussion. Describe the sounds different objects make.

♪ Share Mildred Pitts Walter's *Ty's One-Man Band* (New York: Four Winds Press, 1980). Try making music with a comb, a washboard, wooden spoons, and a pail.

♪ Use clay pots, bottles of assorted sizes and shapes, nails and bolts, aluminum pipes and pot lids, bones, pieces of wood that are of different lengths, and other objects to hang as wind chimes. Experiment with sounds. One musician in Colorado has used wrenches hung from a rod for a wrench chime. For directions for making a wrench xylophone and other instruments, see *Making Music: Six Instruments You Can Create* by Eddie Herschel Oates (New York: HarperCollins, 1995).

♪ Research drums. What other instruments are in the percussion section? Contact an orchestra director and make arrangements to get an introduction to the instruments in a percussion section.

♪ Create your own drums from a variety of materials.

♪ Share Gene Baer's *Thump, Thump, Rat-a-Tat-Tat* (New York: Harper-Trophy, 1989) with younger children. Using the drums and other instruments the children have made, create a parade. Consider using John Philip Sousa music in the background.

♪ Draw a cartoon about a drum.

♪ "Osebo's Drum" is an African story. Can you discover other African instruments? Share what you find with others.

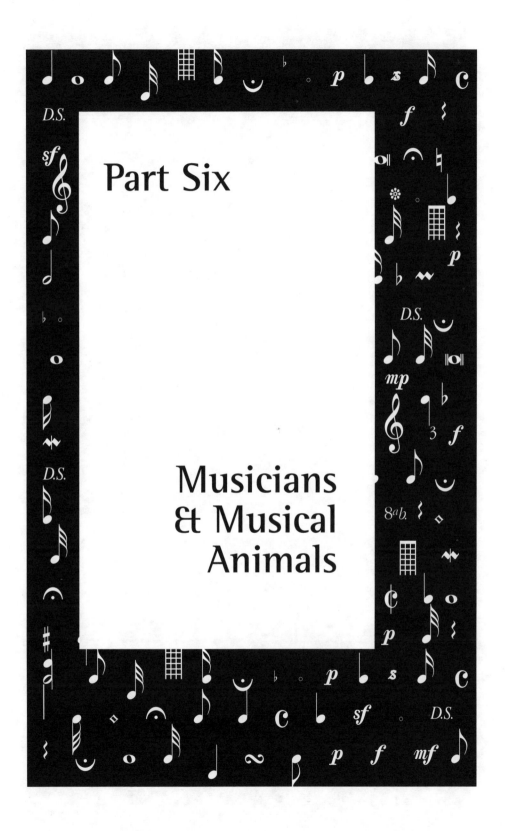

Part Six

Musicians
& Musical
Animals

We are all familiar with "Jack and the Beanstalk." Here is a similar adventure with Jack and the family cows.

The Bee, the Harp, the Mouse, and the Bum-Clock

(Ireland)*

NCE THERE WAS A WIDOW, and she had one son, called Jack. Jack and his mother owned just three cows. They lived well and happy for a long time; but at last hard times came down on them, and the crops failed, and poverty looked in at the door, and things got so sore against the poor widow that for want of money and for want of necessities she had to make up her mind to sell one of the cows. "Jack," she said one night, "go over in the morning to the fair to sell the branny (speckled brown) cow."

Well and good. In the morning my brave Jack was up early, and took a stick in his fist and turned out the cow, and off to the fair he went with her; and when Jack came into the fair, he saw a great crowd gathered in a ring in the street. He went into the crowd to see what they were looking at, and there in the middle of them he saw a man with a wee, wee harp; a mouse; a bum-clock (cockroach); and a bee to play the harp. And when the man put them down on the ground and whistled, the bee began to play the harp, and the mouse and the bum-clock stood up on their hind legs and got hold of each other and began to waltz. And as soon as the harp began to play and the mouse and the bum-clock to dance, there wasn't a man or woman or a thing in the fair that didn't begin to dance also, and the pots and pans and the wheels and reels jumped and jiggled all over the town, and Jack himself and the branny cow were as bad as the next.

There was never a town in such a state before or since, and after a while the man picked up the bee, the harp, the mouse, and the bum-clock and put them into his pocket, and the men and women, Jack and the cow, the pots and pans, and wheels and reels that had hopped and jigged now stopped, and everyone began to laugh as if to break his heart. Then the man turned to Jack. "Jack," says he, "how would you like to be master of all these animals?"

"Why," says Jack, "I should like it fine."

"Well, then," says the man, "how will you and me make a bargain about them?"

"I have no money," says Jack.

"But you have a fine cow," says the man. "I will give you the bee and the harp for it."

"Oh, but," Jack says, says he, "my poor mother at home is very sad and sorrowful entirely, and I have this cow to sell and lift her heart again."

"And better than this she cannot get," says the man. "For when she sees the bee play the harp, she will laugh if she never laughed in her life before."

"Well," says Jack, says he, "that will be grand."

He made the bargain. The man took the cow, and Jack started home with the bee and the harp in his pocket, and when he came home, his mother welcomed him back.

"And Jack," says she, "I see you have sold the cow."

"I have done that," says Jack.

"Did you do well?" says the mother.

"I did well, and very well," says Jack.

"How much did you get for her?" says the mother.

"Oh," says he, "it was not for money at all I sold her, but for something far better."

"Oh, Jack! Jack!" says she, "what have you done?"

"Just wait until you see, Mother," says he, "and you will soon say I have done well."

Out of his pocket he took the bee and the harp and set them in the middle of the floor, and whistles to them, and as soon as he did this the bee began to play the harp. The mother she looked at them and let a big, great laugh out of her, and she and Jack began to dance. The pots and pans, the wheels and reels began to jig and dance over the floor, and the house itself hopped about also.

When Jack picked up the bee and the harp again, the dancing all stopped, and the mother laughed for a long time. But when she came to herself, she got very angry entirely with Jack, and she told him he was a silly, foolish fellow, and that there was neither food nor money in the house, and now he had lost one of her good cows, also. "We must do something to live," says she. "Over to the fair you must go tomorrow morning, and take the black cow with you and sell her."

And off in the morning at an early hour, brave Jack started, and never halted until he was in the fair. When he came into the fair, he saw a big crowd gathered in a ring in the street. Said Jack to himself, "I wonder what are they looking at."

Into the crowd he pushed, and saw the wee man this day again with a mouse and a bum-clock, and he put them down in the street and whistled. The mouse and the bum-clock stood up on their hind legs and got hold of each other and began to dance there and jig, and as they did there was not a man or woman in the street who didn't begin to jig also, and Jack and the black cow and the wheels and the reels and the pots and pans, all of them were jigging and dancing all over the town, and the houses themselves were jumping and hopping about, and such a place Jack or anyone else never saw before.

When the man lifted the mouse and the bum-clock into his pocket, they all stopped dancing and settled down, and everybody laughed right hearty. The man turned to Jack. "Jack," said he, "I am glad to see you; how would you like to have these animals?"

"I should like well to have them," says Jack, says he, "only I cannot."

"Why cannot you?" says the man.

"Oh," says Jack, says he, "I have no money, and my poor mother is very downhearted. She sent me to the fair to sell this cow and bring some money to lift her heart."

"Oh," says the man, says he, "if you want to lift your mother's heart I will sell you the mouse, and when you set the bee to play the harp and the mouse to dance to it, your mother will laugh as she never laughed in her life before."

"But I have no money," says Jack, says he, "to buy your mouse."

"I don't mind," says the man, says he, "I will take your cow for it."

Poor Jack was so taken with the mouse and had his mind so set on it, that he thought it was a grand bargain entirely, and he gave the man his cow, and took the mouse and started off for home, and when he got home his mother welcomed him.

"Jack," says she, "I see you have sold the cow."

"I did that," says Jack.

"Did you sell her well?" says she.

"Very well indeed," says Jack, says he.

"How much did you get for her?"

"I didn't get money," says he, "but I got value."

"Oh, Jack, Jack!" says she, "what do you mean?"

"I will soon show you that, mother," says he, taking the mouse out of his pocket and the harp and the bee and setting all on the floor; and when he began to whistle, the bee began to play, and the mouse got up on its hind legs and began to dance and jig, and the mother gave such a hearty laugh as she never laughed in her life before. To dancing and jigging herself and Jack fell, and the pots and pans and the wheels and reels began to dance and jig over the floor, and the house jigged also. And when they were tired of this, Jack lifted the harp and the mouse and the bee and put them in his pocket, and his mother she laughed for a long time.

But when she got over that she got very downhearted and very angry entirely with Jack. "And oh, Jack," she says, "you are a stupid, good-for-nothing fellow. We have neither money nor meat in the house, and here you have lost two of my good cows, and I have only one left now. Tomorrow morning," she says, "you must be up early and take this cow to the fair and sell her. See to get something to lift my heart up."

"I will do that," says Jack, says he. So he went to his bed, and early in the morning he was up and turned out the spotty cow and went to the fair.

When Jack got to the fair, he saw a crowd gathered in a ring in the street. "I wonder what they are looking at, anyhow," says he. He pushed through the crowd, and there he saw the same wee man he had seen before with a bum-clock; and when he put the bum-clock on the ground, he whistled, and the bum-clock began to dance, and the men, women, and children in the street, and Jack and the spotty cow began to dance and jig also, and everything on the street and about it, the wheels and reels, the pots and pans, began to jig, and the houses themselves began to dance likewise. And when the man lifted the bum-clock and put it in his pocket, everybody stopped jigging and dancing and every one laughed loud. The wee man turned and saw Jack.

"Jack, my brave boy," says he, "you will never be right fixed until you have this bum-clock, for it is a very fancy thing to have."

126

"Oh, but," says Jack, says he, "I have no money."

"No matter for that," says the man, "you have a cow, and that is as good as money to me."

"Well," says Jack, "I have a poor mother who is very downhearted at home, and she sent me to the fair to sell this cow and raise some money and lift her heart."

"Oh, but Jack," says the wee man, "this bum-clock is the very thing to lift her heart, for when you put down your harp and bee and mouse on the floor, and put the bum-clock along with them, she will laugh as she never laughed in her life before."

"Well, that is surely true," says Jack, says he, "and I think I will make a swap with you."

So Jack gave the cow to the man and took the bum-clock himself, and started for home.

His mother was glad to see Jack back, and says she, "Jack, I see that you have sold the cow."

"I did that, Mother," says Jack.

"Did you sell her well, Jack?" says the mother.

"Very well indeed, Mother," says Jack.

"How much did you get for her?" says the mother.

"I didn't take any money for her, Mother, but value," says Jack, and he takes out of his pocket the bum-clock and the mouse, and set them on the floor and began to whistle, and the bee began to play the harp and the mouse and the bum-clock stood up on their hind legs and began to dance, and Jack's mother laughed very hearty, and everything in the house, the wheels and the reels, and the pots and pans, went jigging and hopping over the floor, and the house itself went jigging and hopping about likewise.

When Jack lifted up the animals and put them in his pocket, everything stopped, and the mother laughed for a good while. But after a while, when she came to herself, and saw what Jack had done and how they were now without either money, or food, or a cow, she got very, very angry at Jack, and scolded him hard, and then sat down and began to cry.

Poor Jack, when he looked at himself, confessed that he was a stupid fool entirely. "And what," says he, "shall I now do for my poor mother?" He went out along the road, thinking and thinking, and he met a wee woman who said, "Good-morrow to you, Jack," says she, "how is it you are not trying for the king's daughter of Ireland?"

"What do you mean?" says Jack.

Says she, "Didn't you hear what the whole world has heard, that the king of Ireland has a daughter who hasn't laughed for seven years, and he has promised to give her in marriage, and to give the kingdom along with her, to any man who will take three laughs out of her."

"If that is so," says Jack, says he, "it is not here I should be."

Back to the house he went, and gathers together the bee, the harp, the mouse, and the bum-clock, and putting them into his pocket, he bade his mother good-by, and told her it wouldn't be long till she got good news from him, and off he hurries.

When he reached the castle, there was a ring of spikes all round the castle and men's heads on nearly every spike there.

"What heads are these?" Jack asked one of the king's soldiers.

"Any man that comes here trying to win the king's daughter, and fails to make her laugh three times, loses his head, and has it stuck on a spike. These are the heads of the men that failed," says he.

"A mighty big crowd," says Jack, says he. Then Jack sent word to tell the king's daughter and the king that there was a new man who had come to win her.

In a very little time the king and the king's daughter and the king's court all came out and sat themselves down on gold and silver chairs in front of the castle, and ordered Jack to be brought in until he should have his trial. Jack, before he went, took out of his pocket the bee, the harp, the mouse, and the bum-clock, and he gave the harp to the bee, and he tied a string to one and the other, and took the end of the string himself, and marched into the castle yard before all the court, with his animals coming on a string behind him.

When the queen and the king and the court and the princes saw poor, ragged Jack with his bee and mouse and bum-clock hopping behind him on a string, they set up one roar of laughter that was long and loud enough, and when the king's daughter herself lifted her head and looked to see what they were laughing at, and saw Jack and his paraphernalia, she opened her mouth and she let out of her such a laugh as was never heard before.

Then Jack drops a low curtsy and says, "Thank you, my lady; I have one of the three parts of you won."

Then he drew up his animals in a circle, and began to whistle, and the minute he did, the bee began to play the harp, and the mouse and the bum-clock stood up on their hind legs, got hold of each other, and began to dance, and the king and the king's court and Jack himself began to dance and jig, and everything about the king's castle, pots and pans, wheels and reels, and the castle itself began to dance also. And the king's daughter, when she saw this, opened her mouth again, and let out of her a laugh twice louder than she let before, and Jack, in the middle of his jigging, drops another curtsy, and says, "Thank you, my lady; that is two of the three parts of you won."

Jack and his menagerie went on playing and dancing, but Jack could not get the third laugh out of the king's daughter, and the poor fellow saw his big head in danger of going on the spike. Then the brave mouse came to Jack's help and wheeled round upon its heel, and as it did so its tail swiped into the bum-clock's mouth, and the bum-clock began to cough and cough and cough. And when the king's daughter saw this she opened her mouth again, and she let the loudest and hardest and merriest laugh that was ever heard before or since; and, "Thank you, my lady," says Jack, dropping another curtsy; "I have all of you won."

Then when Jack stopped his menagerie, the king took him and the menagerie within the castle. He was washed and combed, and dressed in a suit of silk and satin, with all kinds of gold and silver ornaments, and then was led before the king's daughter. And true enough, she confessed that a handsomer and finer fellow than Jack she had never seen and she was very willing to be his wife.

Jack sent for his poor old mother and brought her to the wedding, which lasted nine days and nine nights, every night better than the other. All the lords and ladies and gentry of Ireland were at the wedding. I was at it, too, and got brogues, broth, and slippers of bread and came jigging home on my head.

*From Irish Fairy Tales, edited by Philip Smith (New York: Dover Publications, 1993); taken from Donegal Fairy Stories, 1900. Reprinted by Dover Publications (ISBN 0-486-21971-2).

This is a typical whopper about some amazing, unique musicians.

The Musical Mice

(United States)

FELLOW WENT INTO A BAR, swung his bottom on a bar stool and had a couple of drinks. "Do you want to see something?" he asked the bartender.

The bartender shrugged his shoulders and said, "I've seen lots of things. Why not?"

The fellow fished in his coat pocket and took out something wrapped in a handkerchief. He unfolded it and laid out a tiny piano and a stool on the bar.

"That's something!" said the bartender.

"Wait, wait, wait. You haven't seen the rest of it," said the fellow. He reached ever so carefully into his shirt pocket and took out a tiny mouse and he sat the mouse down on the piano stool and said, "Play."

The mouse started to beat out Rachmaninoff, Bach, Brahms, and Beethoven.

"Now that's really different. I have never seen anything like this. It is wonderful," said the bartender, who was really a lover of great music.

People got up from their chairs and stools and crowded around the fellow to get a good view of what was going on.

"You ain't seen anything yet," bragged the fellow.

He reached into his vest pocket and got out another mouse. He put it next to the piano and said, "Sing."

The little mouse pianist beat out the rhythm and the singing mouse sang the aria from the opera *Carmen*. Next the mouse sang the aria from *The Magic Flute*.

Everyone gathered around at the bar was thunderstruck. Someone said, "Do you know, that's the most amazing thing I've ever seen in all my born days? I'll give you thirty thousand dollars for the mice and piano. I'll give it to you in cash right now. I just won that much at a card game."

The bartender whispered to the fellow, "Don't sell it. What you have is worth more than a million dollars. You could make a fortune with it on television."

The fellow looked at the bartender and said, "Aw, I'm going to sell it. I need the money right now."

It was a deal and the card player handed over thirty thousand dollars to the fellow. After that, the card player picked up the two mice and the piano and left the bar.

"Boy, you are really crazy. You could have made a lot more money than thirty thousand with those mice and the piano," roared the bartender.

"Aw, shucks, don't be silly. It's really a phony," laughed the fellow.

"What do you mean, it's a phony?" asked the bartender.

"That mouse can't sing! The one at the piano is a ventriloquist!" answered the fellow as he put the wad of money in his pants pocket.

There are many ways to make music!

The Singing Frogs

(China)*

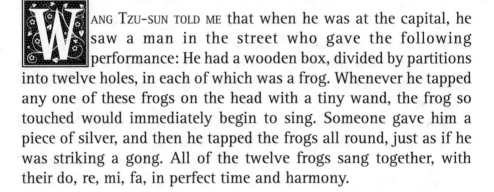ANG Tzu-sun TOLD ME that when he was at the capital, he saw a man in the street who gave the following performance: He had a wooden box, divided by partitions into twelve holes, in each of which was a frog. Whenever he tapped any one of these frogs on the head with a tiny wand, the frog so touched would immediately begin to sing. Someone gave him a piece of silver, and then he tapped the frogs all round, just as if he was striking a gong. All of the twelve frogs sang together, with their do, re, mi, fa, in perfect time and harmony.

*Taken from Stories from a Chinese Studio, *translated and annotated by Herbert A. Giles (New York: Dover Publications, 1969).*

Music has led to feverish dancing activities and dancing compulsions. For another story of compulsive dancing, read or listen to Hans Christian Andersen's story "The Red Shoes."

The Shoes That Were Danced to Pieces

(Germany)*

NCE UPON A TIME, there was a king who had twelve daughters, each more beautiful than the other. They all slept together in one chamber, in which their beds stood side by side, and every night when they were in their beds, the king locked the door and bolted it. But in the morning when he unlocked the door, he saw that their shoes were worn out with dancing, and no one could find out how that had come to pass. Then the king caused it to be proclaimed that whosoever could discover where his daughters danced at night, should choose one of them for his wife and be king after his death; but that whosoever came forward and had not discovered it within three days and nights, should have forfeited his life.

It was not long before a king's son presented himself, and offered to undertake the enterprise. He was well received, and in the evening was led into a room adjoining the princesses' sleeping chamber. His bed was placed there, and he was to observe where they went and danced, and in order that they might do nothing secretly or go away to some other place, the door of their room was left open.

But the eyelids of the prince grew heavy as lead, and he fell asleep When he awoke in the morning, all twelve daughters had been to the dance, for their shoes were standing there with holes in the soles. On the second and third nights it fell out just the same, and then the prince's head was struck off without mercy. Many others came after this and undertook the enterprise, but all forfeited their lives.

Now it came to pass that a poor soldier who had a wound and could serve no longer, found himself on the road to the town where the king lived. There he met an old woman, who asked him where he was going. "I hardly

133

know myself," answered he, and added in jest, "I had half a mind to discover where the princesses dance their shoes into holes, and thus become king."

"That is not so difficult," said the old woman, "you must not drink the wine which will be brought to you at night, and must pretend to be sound asleep."

With that she gave him a little cloak, and said, "If you put on that, you will be invisible, and then you can steal after the twelve."

When the soldier had received this good advice, he went into the thing in earnest, took heart, went to the king, and announced himself as a suitor. He was as well received as the others, and royal garments were put upon him. He was conducted that evening at bedtime into the antechamber, and as he was about to go to bed, the eldest daughter came and brought him a cup of wine, but he had tied a sponge under his chin, and let the wine run down into it, without drinking a drop. Then he lay down and when he had lain a while, he began to snore, as if in the deepest sleep.

The twelve princesses heard that and laughed, and the eldest said, "He, too, might as well have saved his life." With that they got up, opened wardrobes, presses, and cupboards, and brought out pretty dresses. They dressed themselves before the mirrors, sprang about, and rejoiced at the prospect of the dance. Only the youngest said, "I know not how it is; you are very happy, but I feel very strange; some misfortune is certainly about to befall us."

"You are a goose, who is always frightened," said the eldest. "Have you forgotten how many kings' sons have already come here in vain? I had hardly any need to give the soldier a sleeping draught; in any case, the clown would not have awakened."

When they were all ready, they looked carefully at the soldier, but he had closed his eyes and did not move or stir, so they felt themselves quite secure. The eldest then went to her bed and tapped it; it immediately sank into the earth, and one after the other they descended through the opening, the eldest going first.

The soldier, who had watched everything, tarried no longer, put on his little cloak, and went down last with the youngest. Halfway down the steps, he trod just a little on her dress; she was terrified at that and cried out, "What is that? Who is pulling at my dress?"

"Don't be so silly!" said the eldest, "you have caught it on a nail." Then they went all the way down, and when they were at the bottom, they were standing in a wonderfully pretty avenue of trees, all the leaves of which were of silver and shone and glistened.

The soldier thought, "I must carry a token away with me," and broke off a twig from one of them, upon which the tree cracked with a loud report.

The youngest cried out again, "Something is wrong, did you hear the crack?"

But the eldest said, "It is a gun fired for joy, because we have got rid of our prince so quickly." After that they came into an avenue where all the leaves were of gold, and lastly into a third avenue where they were of bright diamonds. The soldier broke off a twig from each, which made such a crack each time that the youngest started back in terror, but the eldest still maintained that they were salutes.

They went on and came to a great lake whereon stood twelve little boats, and in every boat sat a handsome prince, all of whom were waiting for the twelve, and each took one of them with him, but the soldier seated himself by the youngest.

Then her prince said, "I can't tell why the boat is so much heavier today; I shall have to row with all my strength if I am to get it across."

"What should cause that," asked the youngest, "but the warm weather? I feel very warm too."

On the opposite side of the lake stood a splendid, brightly lit castle, from whence resounded the joyous music of trumpets and kettledrums. They rowed over there, entered, and each prince danced with the girl he loved, but the soldier danced with them unseen, and when one of them had a cup of wine in her hand he drank it up, so that the cup was empty when she carried it to her mouth. The youngest was alarmed at this, but the eldest always made her be silent.

The music was enchanting and called them to dance. They danced there till three o'clock in the morning when all the shoes were danced into holes, and they were forced to leave off. The princes rowed them back again over the lake, and this time the soldier seated himself by the eldest. On the shore they took leave of their princes, and promised to return the following night. When they reached the stairs the soldier ran on in front and lay down in his bed, and when the twelve had come up slowly and wearily, he was already snoring so loudly that they all could hear him. They said, "So far as he is concerned, we are safe." They took off their beautiful dresses, laid them away, put the worn-out shoes under the bed, and lay down.

Next morning, the soldier was resolved not to speak, but to watch the wonderful goings on, and again went with them. Everything was done just as it had been done the first time and each time they danced to the bewitching music until their shoes were worn to pieces.

The third time he took a cup away with him as a token. When the hour had arrived for him to give his answer, he took the three twigs and the cup and went to the king. The twelve stood behind the door and listened for what he was going to say.

When the king put the question, "Where have my twelve daughters danced their shoes to pieces in the night?" he answered, "In an underground castle with twelve princes," and related how it had come to pass and then brought out the tokens.

The king summoned his daughters and asked them if the soldier told the truth. When they saw that they were betrayed and that falsehood would be of no avail, they were obliged to confess all. Thereupon the king asked the soldier which of them he would have to wife.

The soldier answered, "I am no longer young, so give me the eldest." The wedding was celebrated on the selfsame day, and the kingdom was promised him after the king's death.

Collected by Jacob Grimm and Wilhelm Grimm.

Whistling, singing, and dancing are featured in this New England story.

The Dancing Sheriff
(United States)

HE SHERIFF WAS KNOWN for being hard-hearted and incapable of pity for anyone. And right now, he was out to bring Old Man Elias to justice.

Old Man Elias worked hard in the fields to keep his home together. He often told people he didn't even have enough money to buy scissors to trim his long, flowing white beard. He explained to everyone that even though he was so poor and had few belongings, he was rich in hearing and making music. He was always whistling, humming, or singing in his creaky, crackly old voice. If his beard hadn't been such a tangled mess (he didn't have the money to buy a comb either), the smile on his face would have been seen as he hummed to himself.

One hot, steamy summer day, Old Man Elias was out in the meadow cutting the hay. The sun was beating down and he was sweating big drops of sweat from his brow, his face, his neck, right down to his arms and hands. Through it all, though, he was whistling an old country tune.

The sheriff found him in the field and ordered him, "Old Man Elias! Stop whistling long enough to hear me. You owe three dollars for Old Tom's pig, and if you don't pay it up right now, I'll take you straight to jail."

"Hey," said Old Man Elias, "I don't owe three dollars to no one, especially Old Tom. The pig wasn't any good, and anyone who claims it was is lying. Besides, I ain't got three dollars, so I couldn't pay even if I had a mind to!" Old Man Elias thought that ended it all and went back to his whistling and cutting the hay.

It wasn't going to be that easy, though. The sheriff was in a particularly hard-hearted mood. "Then to jail you go, you darn old whistler!"

137

"I ain't fond of the thought of going to jail, but if that is what it takes, off I'll go," Old Man Elias muttered. "Before I go to jail, though, I need to go to the squire to collect the money he owes me for cutting the hay in the meadow."

They marched right off to the squire's place. The squire reached into his pocket and brought out five shiny new silver dollars that he gave to Old Man Elias. "There you go then," said the squire. "You did a good job of it, I am sure, like you always do."

"Well now," pondered the frustrated sheriff. "Now, you have enough money to pay the three dollars. You are lucky that you can stay out of jail," said the sheriff, who was really frustrated that Old Man Elias had managed to get the money.

"Nope," Elias said. "Off to jail I go. I told you before, the pig was no good and I don't owe any three dollars. Besides, I need the five silver dollars so's I can eat while I'm in jail."

He began to trudge along the road toward jail. The road was dusty and the sun was hot, but Old Man Elias started humming as he bent his head and trudged.

"Hell's bells and little fish hooks," exclaimed the red-faced sheriff. "If you are not in jail, you won't have to eat in it. Truth is you don't have to be in jail if you only give me the three dollars and call it done."

Old Man Elias stopped his humming. "Nope! To jail you said I have to go and so I'll darn-tooting go to jail. I can't pay you because I'll need to spend my five silver dollars for food."

The sun was beating straight down and the day was getting sweltering hot. The road was long and dusty. Little gusts of wind caught the dust into small dust devils. Even mean-hearted sheriffs get tired and hungry, and the sheriff was just that. "You are walking so slow, Old Man Elias, that we won't reach the jail for at least another day. Can't you hum a sprightly tune?"

Then the sheriff snorted and sort of whined, "I never meant to take you to jail. I only said that to get three easy dollars. You don't have to go to jail. On top of that I have an errand to do on the opposite road."

"You arrested me, sheriff. Let's get on our way to jail. Maybe it will be cool in there," said Old Man Elias.

"Now, look you stubborn old whistler," begged the sheriff. "Get you along on home now. I have someplace to go where I'll probably gain something. The only thing I can gain from you is a sore ear listening to your whistling and humming. To say nothing of your creaky singing!"

"You can't make a fool of me, sheriff," replied Old Man Elias. He even put "No, you can't make a fool of me" into a song he sang. "I'm not a crook, so off to jail I go."

Old Man Elias sang his new song, "No, you can't make a fool of me," as they dragged their feet in the dusty road.

Did I remember to tell you that the sheriff was stout? Heck, he was downright fat and he was sweating like a full kettle boiling and bubbling on a cold day. The more he sweated, the more the flies landed on him and bit him and the sweat bees zipped in and out around him.

They came to a bridge that ran over a deep river. Across the river on the other side of the bridge the road forked. The fork to the right went to the jail, but the left fork was the road the sheriff wanted to take. The sheriff stopped and mopped his brow.

"Old Man Elias, go back home. I'll say it again. You don't have to go to jail. Go home," ordered the sheriff.

"That wouldn't be right. You came to take me to jail and so it's to jail I'm going," argued Old Man Elias.

"Look, Elias, I'm begging you. Don't go to jail," pleaded the sheriff.

Then a look of pure pleasure came into Old Man Elias's eyes. "Maybe since you are begging, I'll do what you say, but first, you have to do something for me. You know our local belief that seeing a sheriff dancing on a bridge with water running under it will bring good luck for a year and a day. I could use some good luck. You saw me, an old man working out in the hot sun for money. If you dance on the bridge while I sing "Old Chalmouny Fair" I'll go home and not to jail. You can go your way and I'll take my year of luck home with me."

The sheriff blustered and stammered. "Hell's bells and little fish hooks! You have honey on your brain if you think I would dance on the bridge."

"Then I'll just have to go straight to jail. I didn't think you would begrudge an old man a little bit of luck," wheedled Old Man Elias.

When the sheriff decided that there was no way around this bridge dance, he looked all around to make sure no one would see this. He walked onto the wooden bridge. He stood there, oozing sweat, until Old Man Elias began singing "Old Chalmouny Fair" in his creaky old voice. The sheriff started dancing while the sun beat down, the flies bit, and the bees stung. The sheriff hopped up and down in his heavy boots while Old Man Elias just kept singing his song.

All the critters, along with one or three farmers passing on the road, had a grand old time seeing this sight. It was a rare and unusual spectacle that hasn't been seen before or since. There in broad daylight, the sheriff stomped and hopped on the bridge.

The singing finally stopped. "I am only stopping the singing because I am tired," chortled Old Man Elias. "I am going to go home now. Thanks for bringing me luck for a year and a day. I hope you have the same kind of luck for a year and a day too. In fact, I hope you have that kind of luck every year. You deserve it for not taking an honest man to jail."

With that, Old Man Elias turned around and started walking back the way they had come. As he walked he sang "Garry Owen."

This story explains why men dance as they do and why women dance as they do.

The Dance of the Monkey and Sparrow

(Japan)

IN JAPAN A LONG TIME AGO, there was an old woodcutter who had to travel farther and farther from his home to find wood. On this day he had to travel so far into the mountains that he got lost. At first he tried to study where he was to see which way to return home, but there were no clues. He was hopelessly lost. He walked for a long time until he suddenly heard the sounds of music in the distance. He also smelled the odors of food and realized he was quite hungry.

He painfully climbed to the top of a hill and there he saw a great crowd of monkeys eating, dancing, and singing. They were also drinking wine that they had made from rice. Everything smelled so good that the old man was filled with a need for food and drink.

The dance and music of the monkeys was so beautiful that it surprised the old man. Then from where he was watching, he saw one monkey pick up a bottle made from a gourd. The monkey filled it with wine and said that it was time for him to be going home. The other monkeys said goodbye as he left.

When the old woodcutter saw this, he decided to follow the monkey and try to get some of the wine for himself.

As the monkey traveled, the gourd-bottle grew quite heavy. The monkey stopped and carefully poured some of the wine into a jar. Then he hid the gourd and the rest of the wine in the hollow of an old tree that had an owl living in it. He put the jar on his head and went merrily on his way again, very carefully balancing the jar.

The woodcutter had seen all of this, and when the monkey was gone, he said to himself, "Ha! Surely he won't mind if I borrow just a bit of that wonderful wine." So he scooted to the hollow tree and filled a jar he found there with some of the wine. The owl watched him and blinked and gently said, "Whooo."

"This is wonderful," he thought as he smelled it. "It is very fine indeed. I'll take some of this back to my wife. Now my problem still is to find my way home."

While all of this was happening, his wife was having her own adventure. She was washing clothes under a tree and suddenly noticed that the sparrows seemed to be having some kind of a party. They were drinking something that smelled very good. She had never smelled anything like it, so she decided that she just had to have some of it.

When the sparrows had finished dancing and singing, the woodcutter's wife quickly tucked one of the gourd-bottles under her robe and scurried home. "I'll take this to my hardworking husband," she thought. "If it tastes as good as it smells, it must be extremely fine. Oh, how he will enjoy it after all of his hard work."

The old woodcutter had just found his way home when she returned. "I have something for you," each of them said at the same time. They told each other their stories and exchanged their bottles and each sipped the wine.

Oh, but it was delicious! However, no sooner had they drunk it than they both felt an irresistible urge to dance and sing. The woodcutter's wife began to chatter and jump around like a monkey while her husband held his hands out and chirped and flitted like a sparrow.

The woodcutter sang:

> One hundred sparrows dance in the spring!
> Chirp-a-flit, chirp-a chirp, ching!

While he was doing this, his wife sang:

> One hundred monkeys making a clatter,
> Chatter-chat, chatter-chat, chatter.

The two of them made such a noise that the man who owned the forest they lived in heard them and came running to see what was going on. To his amazed eyes, he saw the woodcutter's wife dancing and acting like a monkey while her husband was dancing and acting like a sparrow. "Here, here!" he commanded. "This kind of behavior will never do. If you must dance, a woman's dance should be graceful and light and ladylike, in fact like a sparrow's dance. A man should dance boldly and with manly strength like a monkey's dance. You two have it all wrong."

So the dancing couple stopped and told their landlord what had happened. "Well, of course," he said. "You have been drinking the wrong wine. Change your bottles and drink again and let's see what happens."

And so after that, the woodcutter always drank the monkey wine and danced in a very manly way, while his wife drank the sparrow wine and always danced in a very ladylike manner. Everyone who saw them dance and heard them sing thought that they were very lovely and delightful so they all began to imitate them. And that is why to this very day men leap about nimbly and boldly while women are much more graceful and birdlike when they dance.

Have you ever seen a mouse dancing?

Where the Mice Danced

(United States)*

ONE DAY THE LITTLE MICE were having a dance. They were dancing in an elk skull. Wihio came walking along over the prairie, and heard the singing, but could not tell from whence it came. He listened, and for a long time looked everywhere to find the singers. At last he found the place.

When he found the skull where they were dancing, he got down on his knees and looked into it. He said to the mice, "Oh, my little brothers, let me come in; I want to dance too."

"No," said the mice, "you must stay outside. You cannot come in. There is not room for you here."

Wihio kept begging them to let him come in, but they would not consent. Then he made up his mind that he would go in anyhow. It looked nice in there. A white lodge was standing there, food was being cooked, and preparations were being made for a great feast.

Wihio made himself small, so as to go in the hole at the back of the elk's skull. The hole was small, but at last, by twisting and turning, Wihio got his head in. When he did this, the mice all became frightened, and scampered out of the skull and ran away.

When Wihio saw that no one was left in the skull, he tried to get his head out of the hole, but he could not. His head was stuck fast. For a long time he tried to free himself, but he could not get the skull off his head, and at last he started to go home. He could not see where he was going, and for a long time he wandered about on the prairie, stumbling over stones and buffalo bones, and falling down into ravines, all the time crying.

144

At last he reached the river, and followed it down toward his camp. His children were swimming near the camp, and when they saw him they did not know what it was they saw and they were frightened, and ran home crying. His wife came out of the lodge to see what had scared the children. She saw a person coming with an elk's skull for a head, and she did not know what to think of it. When she heard the person talking, she knew her husband's voice. Then she was angry and got an axe and tried to break the elk skull. While she was trying to break the skull off, she more than once knocked Wihio down; but at last she set him free.

Taken from "Where the Mice Danced" in By Cheyenne Campfires by George Bird Grinnell (Lincoln: University of Nebraska Press, 1962).

Music arouses emotions, and in this story it can lead followers, whether rats or children, to a sad conclusion.

The Pied Piper

(Germany)*

NEWTOWN, OR FRANCHVILLE, as 'twas called of old, is a sleepy little town, as you all may know, upon the Solent shore.

Sleepy as it is now, it was once noisy enough, and what made the noise was—rats. The place was so infested with them as to be scarce worth living in. There wasn't a barn or a cornrick, a storeroom or a cupboard, but they got into it. Not a cheese but they gnawed it hollow, not a sugar puncheon but they cleared out. Why the very mead and beer in the barrels was not safe from them. They'd gnaw a hole in the top of the tun, and down would go one master rat's tail, and when he brought it up, round would crowd all the friends and cousins, and each would have a suck at the tail.

Had they stopped here it might have been borne. But the squeaking and shrieking, the hurrying and scurrying, so that you could neither hear yourself speak nor get a wink of good honest sleep the livelong night! Not to mention that, Mamma must needs sit up, and keep watch and ward over baby's cradle, or there'd have been a big ugly rat running across the poor little fellow's face, and doing who knows what mischief.

Why didn't the good people of the town have cats? Well, they did, and there was a fair stand-up fight, but in the end the rats were too many, and the pussies were regularly driven from the field. Poison, I hear you say? Why, they poisoned so many that it fairly bred a plague. Ratcatchers! Why there wasn't a ratcatcher from John O'Groat's House to the Land's End that hadn't tried his luck. But do what they might, cats or poison, terriers or traps, there seemed to be more rats than ever, and every day a fresh rat was cocking his tail or pricking his whiskers.

The mayor and the town council were at their wits' end. As they were sitting one day in the town hall racking their poor brains, and bewailing their hard fate, who should run in but the town beadle. "Please, your Honor," says he, "here is a very queer fellow come to town. I don't rightly know what to make of him."

"Show him in," said the mayor, and in he stept. A queer fellow, truly. For there wasn't a color of the rainbow but you might find it in some corner of his dress, and he was tall and thin, and had keen, piercing eyes.

"I'm called the Pied Piper," he began. "And pray what might you be willing to pay me, if I rid you of every single rat in Franchville?"

Well, much as they feared the rats, they feared parting with their money more, and fain would they have higgled and haggled. But the Piper was not a man to stand nonsense, and the upshot was that fifty pounds was promised him (and it meant a lot of money in those old days) as soon as not a rat was left to squeak or scurry in Franchville.

Out of the hall stept the Piper, and as he stept, he laid his pipe to his lips and a shrill keen tune sounded through street and house. And as each note pierced the air you might have seen a strange sight. For out of every hole the rats came tumbling. There were none too old and none too young, none too big and none too little to crowd at the Piper's heels and with eager feet and upturned noses to patter after him as he paced the streets. Nor was the Piper unmindful of the little toddling ones, for every fifty yards he'd stop and give an extra flourish on his pipe to give them time to keep up with the older and stronger of the band.

Up Silver Street he went, and down Gold Street, and at the end of Gold Street is the harbor and the broad Solent beyond. And as he paced along, slowly and gravely, the townsfolk flocked to door and window, and many a blessing they called down upon his head.

As for getting near him, there were too many rats. And now that he was at the water's edge he stepped into a boat, and not a rat, as he shoved off into deep water, piping shrilly all the while, but followed him, plashing, paddling, and wagging their tails with delight. On and on he played and played until the tide went down, and each master rat sank deeper and deeper in the slimy ooze of the harbor, until every mother's son of them was dead and smothered.

The tide rose again, and the Piper stepped onshore, but never a rat followed. You may fancy the townfolk had been throwing up their caps and hurrahing and stopping up rat holes and setting the church bells a-ringing. But when the Piper stepped ashore and not so much as a single squeak was to be heard, the mayor and the council, and the townfolk generally, began to hum and to ha and to shake their heads.

For the town money chest had been sadly emptied of late, and where was the fifty pounds to come from? Such an easy job, too! Just getting into a boat and playing a pipe! Why the mayor himself could have done that if only he had thought of it.

So he hummed and ha'ed and at last, "Come, my good man," said he, "you see what poor folk we are; how can we manage to pay you fifty pounds! Will you not take twenty? When all is said and done 'twill be good pay for the trouble you've taken."

"Fifty pounds was what I bargained for," said the Piper shortly, "and if I were you I'd pay it quickly. For I can pipe many kinds of tunes, as folk sometimes find to their cost."

"Would you threaten us, you strolling vagabond?" shrieked the mayor, and at the same time he winked to the council; "the rats are all dead and drowned," muttered he; and so, "You may do your worst, my good man," and with that he turned short upon his heel.

"Very well," said the Piper, and he smiled a quiet smile. With that he laid his pipe to his lips afresh, but now there came forth no shrill notes, as it were, of scraping and gnawing, and squeaking and scurrying, but the tune was joyous and resonant, full of happy laughter and merry play. And as he paced down the streets the elders mocked, but from schoolroom, and playroom, from nursery and workshop, not a child but ran out with eager glee and shout following gaily at the Piper's call. Dancing, laughing, joining hands, and tripping feet, the bright throng moved along up Gold Street and down Silver Street, and beyond Silver Street lay the cool green forest full of old oaks and wide-spreading beeches. In and out among the oak trees you might catch glimpses of the Piper's many-colored coat. You might hear the laughter of the children break and fade and die away as deeper and deeper into the lone green wood the stranger went and the children followed.

All the while, the elders watched and waited. They mocked no longer now. And watch and wait as they might, never did they set their eyes again upon the Piper in his parti-colored coat. Never were their hearts gladdened by the song and dance of the children issuing forth from amongst the ancient oaks of the forest.

*Taken from More English Fairy Tales, collected by Joseph Jacobs; illustrations by John D. Batten (New York: Dover Publications, 1967).

The Wampanoag have a how/why story that explains a rock formation found at Sekonnet Point, Rhode Island.

Wampanoag Legend of the Singer of Sekonnet Point

(United States)

ONG, LONG AGO, when frogs had teeth, people who traveled near what we know today as Sekonnet Point, Rhode Island, often heard the sounds of sweet singing. It was like no singing they had ever heard before and it seemed to come from the shore.

Many a fisherman heard the songs, came to shore, moored his boat, and went to find this singer. These fishermen discovered that the singer of this ethereal music was the Giant Maushope's wife. Maushope had thrown her across Buzzards Bay when she refused to let him change their children into fish. She had landed at this place on the shore and there she sat for years and years, gazing out over the water and singing her sad songs. She exacted a tribute of all who came to hear her music, but in spite of this tribute, many came back as often as they could to hear her.

Her music haunted them. They wished to listen to her songs again and again. One day, however, travelers listened for it in vain. One man went ashore to see what had become of the singer. To his amazement, he found her seated at the same place, but she had turned to stone.

Troubadour's Storybag

Suggestions for Extending Experiences

♪ Select and research details about a musician or composer. Using this material, read aloud information about the musician or composer with appropriate music in the background. Prepare the reading for a family, community, or school performance. This could be part of a "share musicians" theme.

♪ "Peter and the Wolf" by Serge Prokofiev and "Carnival of the Animals" by Camille Saint-Saëns introduce the instruments of the orchestra as part of the story. Find a composition that uses a variety of instruments. Then write your own story that could be used to introduce various instruments as characters in the story.

♪ Maurice Sendak, author and illustrator of *Where the Wild Things Are* (New York: Harper and Row, 1963), says he has to find the "right" music to listen to as he works on his books. The music provides the mood and inspiration for his art. Select one of his books and find or create music he might have listened to as he worked on the book. What might other authors listen to? What would you like to listen to as you write?

♪ Listen to a musical recording and draw whatever comes to your mind while the music plays. A story piece such as Smetana's "Moldau" encourages seeing a story in the sound. Try different kinds of music: jazz, folk, rock, new age, and others. Did the music enhance your art?

♪ After reading "The Bee, the Harp, the Mouse, and the Bum-Clock," find a version of "Jack and the Beanstalk." Develop a chart comparing and contrasting the two stories. Write a third story using the similarities, differences, and some details of your own invention. Is this a good story for storytelling?

♪ Read "The Bee, the Harp, the Mouse, and the Bum-Clock." Find appropriate music for the critters to play as the people and animals dance. What music would you choose to accompany Jack and the three cows as he takes them off to sell them?

150

Index of Folktales